THE BLAKES

THE BLAKES

The Greek Mission

VENKITESH VIJAY

PARTRIDGE
A Penguin Company

ISBN:	Hardcover	978-1-4828-1248-0
	Softcover	978-1-4828-1249-7
	Ebook	978-1-4828-1247-3

Partridge books may be ordered through booksellers or by contacting:

Partridge India
Penguin Books India Pvt.Ltd
11, Community Centre, Panchsheel Park, New Delhi 110017
India
www.partridgepublishing.com
Phone: 000.800.10062.62

CONTENTS

To
My Parents
&
Beloved brother Karthik

He was a wise man who created the God . . .

Plato

PREFACE

M<small>Y FATHER REGULARLY BOUGHT</small> books for me and my brother. I always had a liking for books on history, historic heroes and mythological characters. These books introduced many of the historic events and heroes of our bygone centuries to me. Facts and fictions about these events and heroes fascinated me a lot and most of the times my net browsing ended in such sites giving more information on history and myth. Roman and Greek mythology, the great Greek Gods, their evolution, their powers—all always attracted me and I used to imagine and visualize those Gods using their powers!!

It was a holiday in 2012 and I had nothing to do as I had just completed reading a book borrowed from one of my friends. I spent some time playing some computer game. I also spent some time browsing the net. I was browsing some site linked to Greek mythology and the God of the Olympus, the Zeus. While watching one of the pictures of Zeus, the events that resulted in Zeus becoming the "Father of Gods and Men" came to my mind and I felt like writing something about the God Zeus and his world.

I just wrote a few lines in computer itself . . . a few lines only . . . It so happened that my father found this and asked me "Are you writing something?" I didn't say Yes or No. But that was enough for him to treat it as Yes. I could not express with a few words the support and encouragement provided by him ever since that day till I finished my maiden literary attempt.

As always, my dearest mother also encouraged me with her love and prayers, which I had been experiencing ever since my birth. And the one person who was more excited and proud from the very first day of my writing was none other than my brother.

I wish to express my sincere thanks to Suresh uncle, one of our family friends, who once gifted me a book on history, which I had referred very frequently during my writing.

I also thank Partridge Publishing for their support and guidance in making this book a reality.

I humbly present my first literary attempt to the huge literary world for the acceptance and criticism of readers . . .

Venkitesh Vijay
vvenkiteshvijay@gmail.com

Prologos
(Prologue)

Two middle aged and healthy brothers are in a coma like stage for the past fifteen days.

Only very few knew that they had planned for a trip to Greece a few days back. It was a surprise for all that they were subsequently missing for some days and was later found lying unconscious near an old abandoned building some fifteen kilometers away from their home.

Though both were seen unconscious, their faces were calm, energetic and full of vigor and even the doctors stated that they don't find any problems with them, but for their sleep . . . .

All the family members are expecting them to come to their normal life any moment. They are all wondering what surprise story they will say when they wake up . . . .

But when . . . ? When will they wake up. . . ?

CHAPTER ONE

"Roark Nemesis"

J OHN BLAKE AND ALEX Blake were twin brothers. Their houses were within one compound wall in a suburban village near London. John was married and Alex was not.

John had two children. One of them was studying in the Cambridge University. Second one named Mathew, was studying in school. Both the Blake brothers were Archeologists.

It was a Thursday afternoon when John Blake called out to his twin brother, Alex Blake, that he found a mysterious scroll in a room in an old abandoned building, some 15 kilometers away from their home. Alex, fair and reasonably built and more adventurous among the Blakes, immediately agreed to meet John at the old building in the evening.

As agreed earlier, in the evening, Alex came through the corner into the empty room where John was waiting for him. In the middle, there was a pedestal in which a scroll was kept. His brother, John was standing beside the pedestal. The light from their torches displayed clear carving of some pictures on the scroll. One showed a man with a trident in his hand, and there was another who had shoes with wings on both sides of his legs. They counted the pictures and found that there were a total of 11 pictures of men and women. There was also a carving of a man with a lightning bolt in his hand on the pedestal.

John figured out that the scroll was in ancient Greek. As he had learned ancient Greek for a few months, he immediately tried to decipher it with his limited knowledge. While John was deciphering it Alex was still thinking of the carvings on the pedestal.

"Who were they?" Alex asked himself.

Just then he had a strange feeling. It was as if he heard a whisper near his ears. It said "Follow the horses and live long enough to see me".

He called out to his brother. "Did you hear that" asked Alex.

"Hear what?" John replied.

Alex thought for one second and replied "Never mind".

John returned back to his deciphering while Alex started to think that, maybe John was right. He must be dreaming.

Then John called out to him "Hey, I think I have deciphered the scroll. Come and have a look for yourself."

Alex went near him and they both read the scroll aloud at the same time. "Face the challenge of the sea. Succeeded you shall face the twelve."

"Who are the twelve?" asked both of them at the same time.

Before they could say anything they heard a thud from where the carving of a man holding a trident was there earlier, and suddenly water was rushing from there!

They could not think of anything. They just ran through the way they came in and started shouting for help. If anyone would see them run, they would think that the entire God's wrath had been loose on them.

While running away from the water they accidently took some wrong turns. Soon they were completely lost and didn't know where to go. Just then Alex had that same feeling again that he earlier had in the room where they found the scroll. He was just thinking as he ran. Then he looked on his sides. To his surprise he saw a horse on his left side. He tried to touch it, but his hand went in through the horse as if it was made of water!

He thought 'I have no choice but to follow the horse'.

He called out to his brother and said "John, I know this place. Follow me." Saying this Alex started running behind the horse. John also did the same thing. But he was not able to see the horse! He just followed Alex. John was wondering how Alex could know this place. They have come here for the first time.

They took many turns and just ran through some darkness. At last they saw an opening above them. They acted quickly. They found wedges on the walls around them. They started to climb through it. When they were about to get out of there, the horse disappeared and a huge wave of water came from down and hit them. Alex was about to fall off when John caught his hand just in time.

Later when the flow of water was less, they got out of that place. After spending so much time in the dark place they could not see properly. When they could see properly, they found that they were in front of their houses! They could not believe their eyes. They were at least fifteen kilometers away from their houses when they got into that old building and found out the secret room and the scroll!

They had some snacks and went to Alex's house to discuss what happened earlier the day. While they were discussing for some time, the doorbell rang. Alex went and opened the door. It was one courier agent.

"There's a letter for you, sir" said the agent and gave him an envelope and a long cardboard box. Alex signed some papers and closed the door.

"Whose is it from?" John asked.

"I don't know. It had no name on it. Anyway let's open the letter first." Saying this Alex tear opened the envelope. He read it out aloud:

> Hi, Alex,
>
> Use the contents in the box well. Please accept it as a gift from me. Do not worry if it is lost any time. All you have to do is to say "**Roark Nemesis**" and it will come back to you. There is some money also for you when you are on the move. They are very valuable. Do not spend them too casually.
>
> Hope everybody is well there. And one more thing, what you faced today was nothing. A lot more is yet to come. Take care.
>
> Bye for now.
>
> Your unknown friends,
>
> P & Z

Saying this he stopped reading. A lot of questions came to their mind straight away. Who is P? Who is Z? What could be inside that box?

John then said "Chill out Alex. I will make a milkshake for you. Meanwhile you open the box" and went to the kitchen to make some milkshake.

Alex went in and brought out a scissors to break open the seal in the box. As he opened he was amazed to see a light coming out of the box!

Then slowly the light faded away and he could see what was inside. He could not believe himself. It was a sword created with such a craftwork that nobody could even find any minute fault in it. It also had a brilliantly crafted handle which had a big ruby at its end. Alex could see his own face in it. Alex thought, whoever had made the sword must have devoted his whole life for it.

John had also seen the light from the room. He asked "What is it Alex?"

"You wouldn't believe if I tell you. So come and see for yourself."

He came with a tray in which two glasses of milkshakes were kept.

As soon as Alex touched the sword, a very unusual thing happened there. The sword suddenly split into two!

After recovery from the initial shock, they were into another one when they suddenly heard both the swords speak! They thought that they were hearing sound from somewhere else. But they were mistaken. It did talk and one of the swords said,

"Hi, our names are Roark and Nemesis. How are you? I hope you are fine because we got a tough road ahead. It shall be very late when you wake up and please do not think this to be a dream. This is real. If you ever want to hear me talk just twist the ruby on my hilt. And about the separation of us, you may be wondering. We came apart because of the bond of you brothers. Now for the things that we are about to do next. It is time that we go to Greece! That's where your mission really begins. Goodbye, we shall see later."

All the time when the sword was speaking both John's and Alex's mouth were wide open because of amusement.

By then Mathew had come searching for them.

"Hey dad, why are you taking so long? It's time for us to sleep." Mathew said.

"Yes, I am coming now. I have a few more things to discuss with your uncle." John replied.

Mathew went back and John and Alex started to discuss further.

"Till yesterday I was any normal man you can see around. And now you can say that I am mad and I will surely agree. I know that it doesn't make any sense." Alex said.

"But we both heard the blades speak. We better obey them. Let's book our next flight to Greece. What I am thinking about right now is what should we do with Mathew? I think it will be better to leave him with Max." John replied.

Max was their neighbor and a good friend of theirs.

Alex said "I consider it is a good opinion of you to say that. I think we should now go to sleep. I shall book our tickets to Greece tomorrow."

John went back to his house. He took one of the swords with him believing that it is his own! He tried to test it. He turned the jewel hilt of the sword. And it began to speak in a low voice! It said "Hey can't you let me sleep for some time?"

Quickly, he made it to sleep.

When he reached home he searched for Mathew everywhere and found him in the bed, already asleep. He too was tired of the day's activities and fell asleep as soon as he lay down on the bed.

Meanwhile Alex was also about to snooze. Just like he had said before, till yesterday they were like any man on the street, and now their life had totally been changed. Their life is now a topsy-turvy one. Alas, it was a wonderful, tiresome and shocking day for them.

CHAPTER TWO

"The Drachmas And The Air"

It was very late before they woke up the next morning. Roark was there where they had left it. Alex wished to test it. He told John his intention. He too liked it. He also wanted to try it out again.

Both of them had their breakfast and went to the woods just behind their houses. Alex wanted to check if the sword is nowhere to be found, will it really come back? So he threw his sword towards his own house thinking that, if he threw it towards the forest and if there was no magic, he may lose his sword! He thought; by doing this he can get back his blade even if there is no magic! Then the sword was nowhere to be seen unless they looked for it.

Alex took a long breath and said aloud "ROARK NEMESIS".

He waited. His brother was also looking everywhere to see if he can spot it. But nothing happened!

"Maybe he cheated us, whoever he is or "it" is" said John, who was depressed.

"But the sword did talk to us. It was not a dream at all. That was real after all. Then why would he or it cheat us?" Replied Alex disappointed.

Suddenly they heard a sound as if somebody was piercing the soil. They looked at the direction from where the sound came. Guess what it was? It was old Roark! Alex ran to him and first thing he did was to turn the ruby hilt. The sword then came to life.

It was Alex who yelled then "What the hell were you doing till now? Do you know how much I was nervous because of you? Don't you ever do this sort of mischief again?"

The sword replied "Do you know anything about us, the swords. We also need some rest. You must know that how much I had travelled yesterday! You would have been snoozing all the day if you were me. It was just a bit of rest and you are getting furious at me."

"Alright, alright I am sorry for all that I said to you." said Alex.

"So I guess it's time for practice." said John.

"What practice?" asked Alex.

"Sword fighting, what else?" John said.

"Yeah. Now your brains are flashing. We are going to see some action." Roark said.

Suddenly Mathew was coming to the room, saying "Dad, I have to go to school. The bus has not arrived till now. Can you drop me there, please?"

John was about to make an excuse when Mathew caught his eyes on the swords. He asked Alex "Uncle, where did you get these blades? Can you get me one?"

Alex thought for a while and replied with a smile "It's a rare collection that I got from a friend of mine. He said it is as sturdy as it was before. So we thought to try it out. Then we shall also get some swordplay practice."

Then all of them heard a honking from the gate. Mathew swiftly said "It must be the bus. Bye. See you later."

Mathew said bye and off he went to his school.

They both then got their positions ready and started fighting with the swords.

Alex made a swift move with his sword and John managed to duck quickly. It was John's turn then. He tried to attack Alex on the face. Alex swiftly put his sword in front of his face and started to push. On the other hand John was also pushing his sword down. John then faced an unexpected kick on the leg. Alex had swiped his and then there was John on the ground. Alex then put his sword's tip at John's neck!

Alex stopped and lifted John up. They felt, it was enough practice for both of them. They returned to the house. This time Alex made the tea for both. Both of them were enjoying the tea and were talking about the training fight they just had.

Alex suddenly remembered that the letter they got yesterday had mentioned about some money. He told John about that. Alex brought the cardboard box in. They searched in it. They could not find any money in it. It was empty!

No, wait. John saw something at a corner of the box. Yes, there was something. There was a wedge in there. No there were two wedges in there. He tear opened one of them. There was a circle shaped thing. No it was not something. It was some sort of a coin. He took it out. And there were lot more in it.

He told Alex to bring a pouch. When it was brought he emptied all the coins in to it. Alex took one out. It was not a regular one. It was a bit larger and weighed much more. It had a golden shade. Suddenly Alex and John exchanged glances. It was made of GOLD!!!!!!!!!!!

They could not believe. The whole lot was made of gold. Who would be mad enough to give this to them?

John asked Nemesis and Alex asked Roark about what these coins were called.

At first they giggled. Then they started to laugh as if Blakes were some kind of jokers from a circus who knew nothing. They waited for them to stop. It was a long wait! After some time they stopped. Alex took it as an opportunity. He grabbed them and asked

"Why are you laughing at us? Now tell us what these are called and please do not laugh again. We want the answer quick."

Roark and Nemesis could see that the Blakes were getting angry as they speak. The fun was over.

Roark said "Alright guys cool down. That gold coin is called a Drachma. It is the official money of the Greek Gods and Goddesses. There are the twelve Olympian Gods, which I suppose you know already, because you are archaeologists and John has studied Greek and Greek mythology."

Alex wanted to clear his doubts. He asked "So are you saying that the Gods and Goddesses are alive and are sending me messages."

Roark replied not sounding too happy "This perception is one which I do not want to speak about. I think you will understand soon."

John was curious about what was in the other wedge. He opened it up and took out a big bottle full of tablets. There was an inscription on it. It read '*Use it wisely*'.

By then Alex also saw this and came closer. He took out one and looked at it carefully. A word was carved in it. He read it out aloud as *'Air'*.

He was about to swallow that one when Roark intervened quickly.

Roark said "I think it shall be better for you to eat that outside."

"Alright" Said both of them and went out.

Nemesis asked John to stand a little far from Alex. He thought 'This day doesn't get any better than this'.

Alex took in a large breath and swallowed the tablet. At first he felt nothing. Then he started to feel something in his right hand. It started to feel light. Suddenly out of nowhere there appeared a ball of gas in his hand.

Roark asked Alex to aim his hand at anything and to ask his mind to shoot that ball of gas at his aim. Alex aimed his hand at a tree behind them and tried to shoot at it. He tried a bit and succeeded in it. That ball of gas he was having at his hand shot off at a great speed. Both Alex and John just closed their eyes.

When they opened their eyes they found out that, where there was a tree before, there were just its trunks. The rest of it was lying here and there. The leaves, the branches and all of it were lying near them. It was a total mess.

Roark said that the fun's not yet over. He asked Alex to do some actions that looked like in yoga. As he did so *"Air"* again came near his hands. But this time when he aimed and shot at a tree, air from all around him came and hit the tree! This time even the trunk was not there. It had uprooted the whole tree! But this time Alex felt a bit tired and weak.

Roark said tiredness was because of his first time experience. He promised them that it will never happen again. Alex sat down to have some rest. He was feeling very tired. Then, with all his strength he set off for his house.

To his amazement he found out that he was not walking anymore. He was flying!!!!!!! He looked back. John was still standing there looking at him with astonishment. He figured it out.

He understood that the "Air" was helping him. He told his mind to go to his house. And it just obeyed him silently! It took him to his house and left him there. He made his way to the kitchen and had some refreshments and straight away went to the bed room.

CHAPTER THREE

"The Floating Diamond"

ALEX HAD A GOOD sleep. When he woke up he had a terrible headache. He went to John's place and took some medicines. At that time Mathew was also at home.

Mathew asked Alex what happened to the trees behind the house. Alex bluffed that when the cops were doing a drill they accidently blew the trees off!

Mathew looked a bit confused but accepted that answer and went.

John asked Alex "Did you get some good sleep?"

Alex replied "Yeah, I think so. Listen we must do our best not to tell Mathew anything about the recent happenings. If he knew, he will ask more and if we don't say anything, he might even feel disappointed."

They went to Alex's place to discuss more with Roark and Nemesis. John asked them what the future plan is.

Roark reminded that as said earlier they have to go to Greece.

Suddenly a sound interrupted. It was from Mathew. Alex and John suddenly twisted their sword hilts to make them silent. Mathew came in.

He said "Dad, can I go and have some fun at my friends place?"

John replied "Do you mean David?"

Mathew replied "Yes Dad"

"Alright. I just wanted to know where you were going. Come back before supper." John replied.

"Alright dad." And he burst out of the room. David was Mr. Dean's son.

Alex said "Well that gives us some time to talk."

John said "Let's try and book our tickets to Greece" and started to their computer room. He turned it on and started to search for tickets to Greece through Internet.

Meanwhile Alex took out his history book collection and started to refer it about Greek mythology and Greek Gods and Goddesses. He decided to study in detail about each and every God. When he reached Poseidon, John called him and said

"Hey, I got two tickets for us."

Alex replied "Great. Which flight is it?"

"It's not a flight." answered John.

"Then what in God's name are we going in?" Alex asked.

"I am sorry, Alex. We are going in a ship."

"What?" Alex asked. Alex suddenly lost his cool and closed the book. Hearing the word "ship" made his mind upset.

Alex went into his room to think about it. Alex hated to go in ships because of an incident that happened during his teenage.

Once Alex and his father were going to an island. John and their mother stayed back because they had some work to do. All was going well on the ship and they reached the island.

There was also another archeologist in the ship whom they met first time but became very close friend to Alex's father. He was friendly to Alex too.

They spent all the day together in the island. In the evening as they were returning a man suddenly sneaked out of the party. The others were not aware of this. They continued boarding the ship and the crew members were least bothered about checking if everybody had come or not.

As they were about to reach the mainland, an explosion was heard in one of the lower cabins. The hull of the ship broke apart. The ship started sinking.

Alex and his father were enjoying the view at the top when the explosion took place. They rushed to the place where the lifeboats were kept. They were about to board the boat when Alex suddenly remembered about his father's archeologist friend. His cabin was on one of the lowest ones. He rushed to the lower cabins.

On the way his pants were soaked as the water was rising slowly. By the time he had reached the lower cabin the water was up to his waist. He rushed in and found his friend stuck under a long desk and unable to move himself. The desk was very heavy and Alex thought it would have broken his legs also.

Alex looked around. He found an axe in a glass cover for emergency. He hit the glass with his hand and took out the axe. His hand was bleeding. Still he used all his strength to fully break the desk. A bit by bit it came apart. His elderly friend was badly injured. He could barely walk. He put his hand around Alex's shoulders and started to make himself out. Alex was even feeling slightly proud about his well built body. By then the water was up to their neck. If anyone had been seeing the scene they would surely mistake it for the Titanic movie with other actors!!

They came out after huge effort. When they were up, everybody gave them way because Alex's friend was injured. Alex's father was waiting desperately for them. As his father and his friend got on the lifeboat, Alex's friend suddenly remembered about his collections that he got from the island! Though he was badly injured, he was about to make a run for it when Alex stopped him and said

"You need rest. I shall get it for you."

He replied "Son, I am proud of you. Even if you can't get the whole collection, please bring the necklace with the Shark's teeth and the Trident in the middle along with you. It is a very very rare piece."

Alex made a huge effort to find the necklace. It was a scene anyone can hardly describe. Most of the time, Alex was under water searching for the necklace.

As he was searching he saw something glowing at one corner of the room. He swam to that place. To his surprise, it was the necklace! The trident in it was glowing like anything.

Alex then had an idea. He wore the necklace so that it will not get lost. He frequently came out of the water to breathe. As he was about to come out a whole bunch of some kind of fishes started to surround him! The necklace was still glowing. May be because of the shining necklace, they scattered away! They were nowhere to be seen.

Alex even today doesn't know why the fishes fled the place when they saw the necklace. And Alex still wears the necklace as a sign of good luck.

Anyway, back to the story. Where were we? Ah, yes. Alex then got out of the water and reached the top. There was panic everywhere. Alex searched for the life boat in which his father and friend was waiting when he went down. It was nowhere to be found. He wondered whether they already left or moved to some other place in the sinking ship! He was sure that his father won't just leave him and go.

He searched every nook and corner of the sinking ship. It looked like as if they vanished into thin air. He looked around himself. Many people were heartbroken because their loved ones were already missing.

Suddenly the captain called everybody to his side. He said there weren't enough lifeboats to save everyone. He said it is a sad situation and requested old people, who had already enjoyed life, should sacrifice their life for younger ones. He again said the children in the vessel have a long life ahead. Some of them agreed with it. Some did not. Those who mentally agreed still hoped that some miracle will help them!

But, those who had not agreed could not bear this. However, others pushed them back. Then the people were giving way to the children. Most of the mothers were crying to leave their loved ones. Very soon all the children were in the boats. It took off. Alex still had the necklace with him. He was hoping to see his father and his friend when they reached the shore.

In the life boat Alex met another guy. His name was Jake and was of his age. He said that he was on the ship for a meeting on the island with his dad and mom. But unfortunately, he could not find his father too. He said that he never wanted to leave the ship until he met his father. But some jerks in the ship pushed him in there in the life boat. Then they talked on and on.

Alex also told him his story. He felt sad for the guy. Suddenly Jake took out something from the pocket. It was something shiny. The light from the object even made it impossible to see the thing. Though Alex wanted to see it, he closed his eyes so that it does not harm his eyes. After all, eyes are very precious!

When he slowly got familiar with the light he removed his hands from his face. He took a closer peek at what Jake had taken out. It looked like a pink crystal.

Jake said "This is a very rare piece of diamond. This was why the meeting took place and this diamond is also the reason why my parents drowned. You know, we boarded a life boat before this. This wretched piece of thing put a hole on the life boat as soon as it took off. Someone pulled me up while most people drowned and drifted away. I found this one still floating on the water! I know you don't believe me. But this really did float and I took it before boarding this life boat."

As he said this he was weeping. Alex tried his best to calm him down. But he won't even let Alex touch him. To Alex's surprise, suddenly he started to shout like a lunatic. He pushed Alex with great force. Alex was even afraid to look at his face as he looked very angry. While all were watching he rushed to the side of the life boat and suddenly jumped into the water!

Alex, after recovering from the shock, ran to the side of the boat with others. Jake was nowhere to be seen. He had already drowned. What a tragedy. Alex was very upset.

Alex disappointedly looked at the water for some more time. As he was about to turn back he saw a faint light. He waited. Then he saw the same diamond that he saw in Jake's hands now floating! And it was floating very near to him, as if it wanted Alex to pick it up.

Alex thought that Jake was telling the truth after all and that the diamond has some magical power. But Alex never believed in magic. He simply thought that all of this was some kind of illusion. But the diamond was real and was floating near him! As if someone was forcing him, Alex quickly picked up the diamond and kept it with him before they started rowing again.

In the life boat Alex was longing to meet his dad. He also thought when he reach home he would tell all of this to John and John would envy upon him. Alex soon got sleepy and slept there itself.

Next morning Alex felt someone sprinkling water on his face. The sailor on the life boat was sprinkling water to wake him up. This time Alex woke up startled. He asked the sailor for some water. After some refreshments Alex asked where they were. The sailor's reply was that they have reached shore an hour ago and those who reached early has already left. Anyway, Alex understood that, they landed near to their home town only.

Alex thanked the sailor and got into a cab arranged by him to go home. While going, Alex was feeling slightly uneasy. Why dad didn't wait for him? Or dad is yet to reach shore? Soon he reached his home. He saw a crowd near his house. There was silence everywhere. When he looked closer at the crowd he found out that most of them were his family members.

Alex rushed into the house. His mother was there. She was crying. When she saw Alex, she came running and kissed him so much. Alex asked her what the reason for all the family members there. She did not reply. When Alex forced her, she pointed her finger to her husband's study. Alex was getting more scared every second. Alex found John also crying. He rushed into his father's study. He could not believe his eyes. He thought his eyes must be deceiving him. His father was dead!

Alex could not take it anymore. His most loved one has said bye to life. He was also crying by then.

Soon after this incident his mother also died. Whenever Alex thinks about a ship or sees a ship, his father's tragic death comes to his mind. This is why Alex does not like to hear about ships even today.

Chapter Four

"The First Test"

John went to Alex's room and tried to calm him down. Alex said "There have been many mysterious happenings since we got that scroll. From there itself our adventure had begun and I am not going to give up until I reach the root of it."

John replied "That's the spirit. Now you tell me what we should do till we go."

Alex said "I think we should check out that scroll. We need some expert advice. How about that we take this to Peter? He is an expert at Greek mythology. We will take it to him tomorrow."

John said "That will be a great idea. He might even know if there is something more of that scroll. But we should be careful not to speak any of this to Mathew."

"That is most certainly correct of what you speak of, John." Alex said.

Just then there came a knock. Alex went and answered the knock. When the door was opened, Alex found himself in front of a Police Inspector.

Alex asked him "Hi Sir, Good to see you. I hope we haven't caused any problems."

He replied with a stern voice "Good to see you too. You haven't caused any troubles, but . . . how do I say it."

"Don't worry sir. You can say it no matter whatever it is." Alex said.

The Officer took in a deep breath and said "Sir, we just got a call from Mr. Dean who is the father of David. He said that his son and one of his friends were kidnapped by someone. We assume that it was your kid, sir."

"Who in the God's name kidnapped them?" said John who just got off from his place of comfort with a very shocking expression on his face, which any parent would have if they hear that their son has been kidnapped. Alex stood aside.

The Inspector said "Sir, please try to calm down. We want your cooperation. We want you at Mr. Dean's house now"

Alex noticed that John was seriously upset to hear this. He wanted to calm it down and to avoid the Inspector speaking more to John. Alex had just about the right idea then.

He said to the inspector "Don't you worry, sir. We can get to their place ourselves. Just give us some time. You can wait for us at the place, sir. Thank you." Saying this he almost slammed the door shut right on the face of the Inspector.

Alex went to the window and observed the inspector move into his ride steered away. John was fully upset. He was scared, afraid, sad, angry and what else.

Controlling his emotions he asked Alex "Alex, why did you say to the inspector that we can get to the place ourselves. You know that our sedan is down in the garage broken down" remembering that some lunatic and alcoholic drove his car straight on their car, the other day.

Alex replied "Who said that we are going by our car and why should we go on that when we have our very own personal rides."

John asked "What do you mean?"

Alex replied "Try to remember. You are sure to get it."

John looked past into his memories. Five minutes over. Still, not a word from John. Alex knew that an upset mind won't work.

Out of patience, he asked "Alex, just tell it"

Alex replied with excitement "Gosh, don't you ever observe. Whatever, now listen. I was thinking of . . . . flying. Does it ring any bell?"

John who just seemed to have been woke up from a dream of blankness and curiosity said "Right. I get it now. We are going to Mr. Dean's place by flying. But, um . . . how are we going to do that?"

Alex said with a slight disappointment on his face because his brother is not back to his normal and can't still guess what he was going to say.

"This is getting from worse to worst. First your son disappears. Now you have started to lose your memory. We will discuss that later. Now straight to the point or else we would lose our precious time. Do you remember that when we were practicing with those tablets and then I felt tired and was heading home and then I"

John interrupted "and then you flew straight to home. You want to fly just like that now also, don't you?

Alex replied satisfied "Thank you for filling in the rest of them. Now do you get the idea "Mr. Not in this world" man?"

John replied "Yeah Yeah "Mr. Know everything". And one more thing, we will take Roark and Nemesis with us, just in case."

"Alright" came a quick reply.

Alex then went to get the huge bottle full of tablets. John went to wake up the lousy swords. John found them near the cupboard which was full of the medals which he, Alex and Mathew had got.

He remembered, when as a small kid, Mathew would promise him that he will make him proud and will get many prizes just like his father and uncle Alex has got.

Tears started coming from John's eyes. His son was out there in the wild city. He could be anywhere from the dirty and rotten pig sty alley to the elegant, stylish and tall skyscrapers.

But he did not have time for any of that. He quickly took the swords and returned to the main hall where Alex was already waiting.

He asked "What took you so long?"

John replied in a soft voice "Memories, long lost memories. Let's go. I would like to get those memories back" saying this he made a dash move to the door with Alex behind him.

As they were out Alex said "John, I think we should take off at a plain and vast ground."

"Yeah, you are probably right. I think the courtyard will be the right place." John replied and went out.

Alex followed him. As they reached the courtyard both of them turned the enchanted swords to life. Both the swords started to teach them the actions for flying. They even taught them how to fly in a very simple method which can be used for a quick take off. Roark told them that this can only be applied to those who have already experience in the normal long way of flying which meant that Alex can fly that way but John had to do the long way.

The swords were like their personal trainers. After some time they said that they were almost ready to take off. Little more time and they were ready!

It was Alex's turn first. He did what was to be done and he shot off in to the sky. It took him a bit of a time to come to control his flying. Meanwhile Roark was shouting to Alex to control his fly with his mind.

Then it was John's chance. Poor John! He had to do all the normal and long way of actions to get it right. After he did all of it, he also lifted off gently. But in the same speed that he went up, he came down!

But that did not affect John. He had made up his mind. He tried again and again and at last he succeeded. He was also in the air and joined Alex.

They had strapped their swords to their belts. They both aimed for Mr. Dean's house in their minds. Alex then felt that maybe he should give John some enthusiasm. So he made his mind to go at more speed. He then yelled back to John "Catch me if you can." and shot off.

John also made his mind to do better. But he did not ask it to go at a greater speed, but asked it to go faster than Alex. To bring John back to his moods, Alex some time flew at the front and tried to frighten John by putting a ball of gas in front of him. In response John sometimes made scary face of an animal.

Alex got what he wanted. John was very much back to his normal. Though he was still worried about his son, he was back with energy to find him at the earliest. Finally after some topsy-turvy, zigzag flight they could see Mr. Dean's house from above. They could also see that Mrs. Dean was crying a lot with tears enough to fill thousand lakes!!

But this was very natural, of course. After all, she had lost her only son. Beside her was Mr. Dean who was answering some questions from the police officer who had come to their place.

Alex and John decided to land somewhere nearby as they didn't like anybody seeing them flying in the air. Just imagine! Two men coming down out of thin air! What a great surprise would it be to the people there!

There was a park nearby. They landed there. Fortunately nobody saw them. They went straight to the scene. Mrs. Dean was still crying.

John went straight to the police officer. The officer saw him and was surprised and asked. "I didn't see you coming! OK, leave that. Mr. Dean here claims that he saw the kidnapper and we have some very interesting response when we asked him. Why don't you yourselves ask him?"

After saying this he took John into the house. Meanwhile Alex was helping Mrs. Dean to calm down. Then she stood up, wiped her face and took Alex to a lonely place.

She whispered to Alex "I still haven't told the cops one thing. Do you want to know it? It might come in handy for you."

Alex replied hastily "Yes, We would love it. It shall be handy for us."

She replied with a little low voice "I also saw the kidnapper. When **"it"** saw me **"it"** came close to me and whispered to me."

Suddenly Mrs. Dean started shivering and started saying something in a peculiar tone and tune as if someone else was trying to speak through her. She said **"With our body we survive but die you shall if you dare enter but you do not outlive without it or else you shall perish. Inside the caves that we live lies what you seek within our handless hands."** After saying this she quickly returned to her normal.

She said "Just now what did I tell you. I can't remember. It all sounded very strange to me, but for you it might mean something"

Alex replied hastily turning all his attention to her "Yes, it does. Thanks to you we now have a slight chance of finding our sons. Now if you will excuse me I would now join John who is waiting for me right there."

John was waiting for him impatiently. He wanted to get out of that place straight away. He was feeling very uncomfortable.

As soon as Alex got near him he said "Hey John. I have some . . ."

John interrupted "I want to get out of here right now."

"But what happened there? Come on we have to talk." Alex said and started following John who has already reached the gate by then.

John replied without turning back "We shall talk while flying."

There was no further talk from either of them before they started flying.

But as soon as they took off Alex broke it "Lets fly slowly. Say to me what happened there."

John gave a grunt and said "They invited me inside. The officer started asking details about Mathew. Then . . ."

Alex was eager "Then what"

"Then he asked about Katrina. This was when I got angry and got out." John said depressed.

Katrina was John's wife. She died in a car accident last year. The reason why he got angry was that she died because of a careless police officer. The officer was chasing a thief when he tripped Katrina's car. From then onwards he hates cops.

Alex remained silent for some time and spoke "John, please relax. We have other matters now. We now have a clue which can lead us to Mathew."

As soon as he heard this John's attention turned on Alex. He was not even concerned where he was flying.

Alex continued "Mrs. Dean claims that the kidnapper said something to her. It was '**With our body we survive but die you shall if you dare enter but you do not outlive without it or else you shall not perish. Inside the caves that we live lies what you seek within our handless hands**.' So does it make any sense to you?" Even Alex was wondering how he could remember each words she said earlier without any omission.

John thought a bit and said "Nothing yet. How about you?"

Alex spoke with a sly grin on his face "Thought you would say that. Well, we are in the same boat. Got nothing. We have to go home right now. We shall discuss it there."

They were heading home very swiftly. Just as they were about a few kilometers away from their house, Alex suddenly got that feeling again. Somebody or someone was whispering to him. It said to him 'Don't go home Alex. Didn't you get it? The clue means that you have to go inside the river. The rest you find yourself. Use the bottle. This will be the first and last time that I shall help you.'

When the voice said to him '. . . bottle . . .' the same bottle which contained the tablet which they used to fly just appeared there out of thin air!

Alex caught hold of it and strapped it to himself. He then called John who was then far ahead of him. Alex went at even more speed and at last caught up with him.

"John, stop there. I figured out the clue. We have to go to the river." Said Alex for which John's reply was

"Really! That's very good news and thank you Alex! Then off we go to the river straight away. It's in the opposite direction"

John then did a half summersault and was facing Alex. Alex also made a straight up the air and took a turn backwards just like a pilot does in a fighter jet.

Both of them were very happy. They finally have a chance and a clue to find Mathew. They asked Roark and Nemesis to teach them to fly even faster. They said it was as simple as winking. You just had to concentrate your mind. They did the same and after some ultra super speed flying, they reached the river banks.

John asked "So, what now?"

Alex replied "Ah, Um, I don't know."

"Look inside the bottle."

"Yeah that sounds like a great idea." Alex took a peep into the large bottle.

He was shocked. Inside it not only was there tablets of flying, but there were also tablets in which water and fire were inscribed! He showed it to John. But John was not shocked. He was rather excited!

He took out two tablets and popped one in to his mouth. John then stood in the shallowly waters. Suddenly he started to feel something. He was feeling like weak and tired first. But soon he was slowly feeling better and better and was very much fresh. Alex also popped in one tablet. He also stood in the water. He was also refreshed soon.

Alex then thought of the rest of the puzzle. He asked himself 'What do we need in our life but will cause us death if we enter'

He looked up. He passed on the question to his dad who was watching him from above! No reply, which was natural of course! Alex put his head down depressed.

Though Alex's face went down sadly, suddenly it came up happily. He found the answer. It was in front of him all this time.

Alex was jumping with excitement to tell it to John. "John, I found it. I got it. The answer issssssss . . . water."

He said "But how Alex, how?"

With this question Alex's excitement only increased "According to the clue, the most essential thing we need is water. But if we enter in to this, won't we die or not? Tell me now, John."

"Wow Alex, You figured it out. Let's go in." He was in a hurry and about to leap when Alex blocked him.

"Not so fast. We need to ask Roark and Nemesis for further information before diving in to the water."

Roark and Nemesis said nothing to worry about. No time to waste, John decided and together they jumped in to the water. They still were not sure whether they will drown and Alex was more tensed. But, after some moments, they were walking underwater relaxed as they could breathe in the water also! They were able to see around too as the water was crystal clear.

They started to observe what's around them. Alex took the left side. He could see, with astonishment, some fishes swim past him. John could see almost the same. But, just some different species.

Though their first experience, they knew that there was always a whole bunch of things to see underwater. A horde of fishes swam between them. This almost made them fall on their knees! John put his hands down on the soft river bed to make him give a grip to himself. His right hand instead of touching the sand, struck a rock of some long spiral shape.

He stood up and took a good look at it. Wow, it was not a rock anymore. Or it wasn't from the beginning! It was a shell of some sort. John looked around. There was only one more. He felt funny! Only two of the whole flock! Maybe they were stray, he thought.

But it wasn't that. Suddenly the fused bulb in John's brain started working. The puzzle! The caves! They were mentioning about these. But who lived inside there?

He decided to tell about the shell to Alex. While John was doing all this, Alex was trying to stand up when another swarm of the fishes came and made him fall completely. This time it took him a while to stand up. Though Alex was healthy and well built, he was feeling more tired than John.

Alex was starting to hate being there. He didn't like to fall so often!

As he stood up, he found John waiting for him with some kind of stupid rock in his hands!!

He said "What are you doing with that rock in your hands?" and took it from his hands and threw it down and asked John to move again.

What a coincidence!! It went and struck the other shell lying half buried in the sand. Both the shells then started to grow bigger, which the two heroes did not see at all!!

They were busy talking. "Alex you shouldn't have thrown that shell. It was part of our clue."

"But John, Would you please explain . . ." he couldn't complete. A sound interrupted. It was from below.

Roark said "Guys, I don't want to interrupt but looks like they want to."

He pointed to where the shells were lying. Well, there weren't any more shells there! There were only two six foot Crabs with spears with clotted blood stains on their right hand and a big shield on the other.

Alex thought, only this much adventure and search for them!! He thought nothing to worry about, except the fact that their death was sure. But he also thought, dying even by doing a little fight with the sword means they died as heroes. John also had the same feeling not to surrender! They decided to fight.

They took out their swords and took positions. The Crab on the right side spoke something followed by the other one. As they spoke the whole place started to shake!

Suddenly the water divided like in the 'Ten Commandments' film. The river banks went crumbling down and walls made of bones came in the place! John and Alex understood that they had created an Arena and they were no more standing under water.

Roark said "These crabs are called the Majins. They can take any hideous disguise they want. They are wielders of ice magic. They can be killed only in one way. Their heart has to be stabbed from the front and back at the same time! Not only that, with this it will be dead and the magic power in it will come to the slayers! It simply means that, if you kill them, you can also control ice magic from later. So Yes, It is a pretty hard task."

Alex gulped but had some quick plan "John, I think the only way to destroy this thing is by first distracting it. So we got ourselves a plan here. You first go at the back of this thing. Then try to distract it. By then I shall come in the front. I too will try to distract it. Then it is your chance. You will have to take some water and splash it on its face. It should take a while for it to get back from that shock. Then strike with all your might on my count."

Still they were afraid that both the crabs shall attack them. But fortunately one of the crabs just waved its hands and sat on the chair made with bones that just appeared. Roark said this was their honor of battle. They only fight solo even if their enemies are more! The Majin took its position and was waiting for them to attack.

They moved according to their plan. As always, Alex took the lead. He went to strike the thing. But he was taken aback by surprise with a wham from its shield and went right into the river bed slamming his face!

But he soon recovered from that. Alex got to his feet. He looked at the crab. Though crabs usually don't have shoulders, he found this one has. He swiftly shifted his blade pointing the tip right at its shoulder. His sword could not even make a scratch on it because it didn't even touch it!!

It was just levitating just above Alex's shoulder. Some forces forbid Alex to touch it. He withdrew Roark! He asked him what was this all about.

Roark said "Not to worry. It's just a first strike protection that they have".

Roark also said that though they are very powerful, they will be weaker soon. While Alex was listening to Roark, John was very much in position to attack.

John also tried to strike it, but he also received a blow from its shield.

John was taken by surprise. How could it know his move? It was facing Alex all the time. It was as if it had a sixth sense or something. John thought he will have one more go. He tried once again. Alas, again a failure.

He had to find a solution for this. John looked around for some clues. He then saw the other one just sitting there. Suddenly it struck him!

Yes, why not? Maybe that one was signaling telepathically to the fighting crab. John decided to try once more. This time he kept an eye on the other one too!

As he raised his sword he again got slammed with his shield. But he got what he wanted!!

He saw the thing sitting in the chair murmuring something. John understood that he had to distract this thing first and then attack the other one and again he had to do it very quickly.

For this he thought of something. He had to take control of the water and smash it on both of them. Then Alex can attack it.

He did just the same. Finally the result was success!! He blew water on the face of the one sitting and the other one just went in for a shock. But that was enough. John and Alex knew that it was tired. He signaled Alex.

Alex said "On my mark. 1 . . . 2 . . . 3 attack."

They hit it with all their might. A howl came from it. Just a howl. Nothing else, and it got vaporized. Golden smoke came from it!! It went to the sky and vanished!!

The other one got up from its seat and stood there in front of Alex and John.

Roark and Nemesis both said at the same time "Oh, no. This is not good. Not good at all. They have done a *tiniture* bond. It means that this one shall explode in about any moment."

As they were saying this Alex and John saw a great sight. From the soil, two kids were rising. They recognized their faces immediately. It was Mathew and David. They found them at last. They were just lying there.

They rushed to pick them up. Thank God!! They were alive though unconscious.

Just then they heard a voice. **"You both have passed the test. That was some good fighting. Roark, you have done well guiding them. Your kids won't remember a thing. When you come to Greece, this shall help you. Bye. We shall meet again soon."**

Then a light appeared above them and two keys dropped from it. They did not have enough time to examine it. They each took one of the kids and took off.

That was when Alex remembered about the explosion to happen. People will be attracted. For this he had a brilliant idea. Alex thought it is the right time to try the ice magic which they just got. He used his ice magic and covered the river with a layer of ice. He was sure that, when the explosion takes place, no sound shall come and the ice will melt and everything will be back to normal. It happened as he planned.

He then looked around him. Nobody saw this. That was good.

Alex then caught the glimpse of John flying far holding Mathew. He, holding on to David, flew straight to Mr. Dean's house.

The police had already left. Alex slowly landed there. David's parents were in the lawn. Mrs. Dean was eagerly waiting for some news from Alex. Alex thought that it might be best not to let them find out that he had found him. For that also Alex had an idea. Alex put David on the soft grass and threw a small stone at them! Then he just took off.

The stone went and hit Mr. Dean's neck!! He went to the direction from where it came. He looked about but found no one. He thought that it was a prank by some kid. But at this time!! He was a bit confused.

But, as he was returning his eyes fell on the grass. There was something lying there or someone. He took a closer look. He managed to find out that it was someone. But it was still pitch dark. He could see no more. He asked his wife to bring a torch light.

When she did she was amazed! Not because that it was somebody lying there, she was amazed because it was her own son. Her husband was also stunned to see his son's face through the tall, soft grass!

He quickly went and telephoned the police. The police were not much surprised to hear this because just then only they had another phone call from John that his son was found in the courtyard!! Then they disconnected the phone.

Mr. Dean asked David if he remembered anything. But David said no. The only thing he remembered was playing with his friends.

Same was the case with Mathew too. John told him to have some good rest. But Mathew kept on asking what had happened to him. John said nothing. However, Alex told him that he would tell Mathew everything when he wakes up to his comfort. While Mathew slept, Alex and John packed their bags for going to Greece. They kept their bags at Alex's room so that Mathew wouldn't find it.

Later when Mathew was awake, he had completely forgotten to ask Alex about what happened the previous day. He was fully focused in going to school that day. He had a test that he couldn't even dream of missing.

John was very pleased to know this. This meant that they had a window open which does not close fast!! They have sufficient time to plan. Mathew watched some T.V program while having his breakfast. It was just an omelet, a sandwich and a glass full of orange juice. He ate that up fast, said bye and then left for some time. Soon they have to go to meet Peter.

CHAPTER FIVE

"A Flight To The Future"

ALEX AND JOHN STRAIGHTAWAY went to Peter. When they reached Peter's house, He warmly welcomed them both and took them to the hall. His servant came and laid some cookies on the table and left for kitchen. Though he had a rough voice, Peter welcomed them very warmly, as always.

He asked "So, Blake brothers, what brings you to me?"

Alex took out the scroll from a cylindrical box. Alex then said "We want you to examine this."

Alex handed over the scroll to Peter. He took out his glasses and put them right above his nose as he usually does. He opened the scroll and started to examine it carefully.

But as soon as he started reading it, he shouted at Alex "Who do you think you are, eh? Do you know how much these cookies cost and you are spoiling my sofa. Get the hell out of here, both of you. You and your scroll! I shouldn't have even welcomed you in. Get out before I call the Police."

Alex and John were surprised with Peter's behavior. Even Peter's maid was frightened by the sudden change in her master's behavior. She had never seen her master behave so violently. He was always so nice. She was afraid that he may even kick her out also! And unlike Alex and John, she had nowhere else to go.

Alex and John rushed out in a flash. They took a cab and set on back to home. There were some minutes of silence.

Then Alex spoke "Weird man, don't you think?"

John replied after some seconds "Well, he behaved so nicely at first, and then when he started staring at that scroll, he suddenly turned wild. The scroll did something to him. It made him mad. You are following me, aren't you?"

Alex said in a bit low voice "Yes, I do. Well we can't go to Peter again asking about this scroll. What do we do now?"

"Why say Peter, We can't show this scroll to anybody. It will make them also mad!!I think it is intended that we don't take this to anyone. I guess what we do now is to prepare for our trip."

"What about Mathew, John? We can't just leave him there. If we even do, what excuse will we make? We are going to meet the Greek Gods!!! Is that what you are going to tell him?"

"Ha ha, very funny, Alex. OK. We are not going to leave him alone. We will send him to Max. We will say to him that we were called for an emergency meeting at Greece"

The cab driver was about to get friendly with them. But when he heard them speak about turning people mad with a scroll, he assumed that they both were Magicians or Psychic!! He got frightened and decided not to speak a word till they reached their home. He was afraid that they will turn him also into a mad person!!

John checked his watch and then said to the driver "Faster driver, faster. My son will reach home from school any minute."

The driver's hand shivered and drove it as fast as he could. When they finally reached home, the driver charged them a reasonable fare.

But when John heard the fare, he became furious "So much for this small distance. I will give you only this much." And gave him lesser amount than what the driver had demanded. The driver was really scared to ask anything!!

John started on the way to his home. Alex felt sorry for the poor and frightened driver. He took out his wallet and gave him the balance fare he demanded earlier and said "Don't worry about John. He gets pretty furious sometimes. Just don't mind him."

The driver said thanks to Alex's kind words and drove off. Alex ran after John.

He asked him "Why did you get angry with him? I didn't see any reason."

"I too don't really know. It just came to me suddenly." Said John a bit tired.

They were very glad knowing that Mathew hasn't reached from school yet. They both were tired. Alex took two small bottles of juice. He gave one to John and had one for himself. Just as they had the last sip, the doorbell rang.

Alex went and looked. Just as he unbolted and opened a bit, a black colored smoke came and blew the door open!! Alex fell down on his back. John helped Alex get up.

The black smoke first covered the whole room. Then it started taking the shape of a man. A man with black robe, black suit and black pants stood there!! It just came from nothing other than the black smoke!!

He said in a grumpy and loud voice "Hey, Alex. Hey John. How's Roark and Nemesis?"

Alex replied "How do you know our names? What is your name?"

John then asked "Is it you who gave us Roark and Nemesis?"

For this he replied "Ha ha, three questions, but one answer. I will not say it."

Alex then asked him "Then why did you come here?"

He laughed and said "Well, the big brothers sent me. We know that your trip is on next Saturday and today is only Monday. They can't wait that longer. So, let's make it shorter."

And he took out a small digital watch from his pocket. Alex and John peeped to look. They could see that the watch had no switch in it except a small one on the top. In the screen, there was only today's day and date. No time!

The man told them to hold to his shoulders. Something made them obey him!! As they did, he pressed the small switch.

When Alex and John saw that nothing has happened for some time, they felt confused what next to expect. Alex tried to put his weight into his right leg. That was when he found that he couldn't feel his legs at all. He looked down to see in horror that there were no legs!! There were no legs for the others either!! It was as if it got vanished.

He immediately asked the man. "Hey, what's going on? What happened to our legs?"

Only then John noticed that his legs were also missing.

The stranger replied pleasantly but in a rough voice "I am pleased to know that you did not faint. Most of us have fainted on the first time, you know. This known as *qaster* transportation is really frightening for the first time and boring thereafter. It takes so much time. And your legs have not gone. It's just invisible. Soon all your body will be too." Then the man pressed on the switch a little harder. Then their waists were also invisible.

A ball of gas then started to appear around them. That was when Alex thought of Roark and Nemesis. He asked about them to the stranger.

For that he replied "Oh, yes I forgot about them."

And then he snapped his fingers. They heard a sound from somewhere in the house. They figured out that it was coming from the back. They turned around and saw the two magical swords coming towards them.

Alex and John spread out their hands but their wrists were also invisible. But that didn't matter Roark or Nemesis. They knew that their hands were invisible. They jumped straight into their hands.

The stranger said "All on board, let's go back to the future."

Then all of them were invisible. They couldn't see each other. But they could hear. A light flashed in front of them for a fraction of a second. Then darkness covered up them again. Then they saw a faint light. It slowly became brighter.

After some time the light revealed that both Alex and John were inside a big cab and a driver was driving it. Alex looked around and was amused to find out that he was sitting with John and the stranger was missing. He also noticed that they were wearing some nice clothes. Meanwhile John was looking at the wallet that he found in his pants. He found their tickets and passports in it. He gave them to Alex.

The driver said "We will reach the Airport shortly."

They decided to discuss further at the airport. The driver slowed down the vehicle. When the driver took out the bags they were amazed. Yesterday only they saw in T.V the launching of a new brand of the strongest and lightest bags. They both wanted it but couldn't afford it. Now it was their own! Alex and John didn't know that it really happened four days back. They never knew that they are already in the future by then.

There were other two small bags also. They paid the driver generously and went into the airport. They gave their bags and took the other two bags as cabin luggage. They passed the security check and other routine things. They went to the waiting place. Their plane was not due for another one hour. They asked a gentleman nearby what day it was. He said it was Saturday.

Alex said "Gosh, this is the future or we missed few days."

John replied, as if he knew it earlier "Yeah. Let's see what's in our bags."

Alex opened his first. He found the bottle of tablets, a purse full of currencies of countries all over the world. China, Russia, Greece, Paris, India, USA, England and some other countries also. Then he found some clothes. And underneath it was Roark!

In John's bag also he found the purse full of money. There was also Nemesis underneath the clothes. The other thing that he found was the packet full Drachmas!

It was then that occurred to Alex that they were about to go in a ship and not a plane. He told John. He was also shocked.

Just then they heard a voice from above 'Alex, John we have cancelled your tickets for going by ship. It would be better for you to go by plane and Mathew is staying at Max's place. We have convinced them that you both are on an expedition and that you both will be back in a week.'

They sighed in relief. Then they heard an announcement. 'The plane going from London to Athens will take off in 15 minutes. It's an early departure.'

They went to the boarding gate and passed all the checking process and boarded the plane. The plane took off smoothly. While flying, there was no problem at all except for some minor turbulence. John fell asleep soon after some time.

Alex had got the window seat. He was just looking outside the window. There wasn't much to see. So soon he also fell asleep. The next thing he knew was John waking him up. "Wake up. We will reach Greece soon."

Just after some minutes they landed. They got off, got their bags, and went out. They saw many people with little papers and placards on which names were written.

John said "No need to look around here. Who is going to come looking for us?"

Alex was about to go when he noticed one of the placards. It had their names on it!!

Alex stopped John and said "John, wait. Look. That man right there is carrying the board with our names. Let's go and ask him."

They went to the man. As they reached near him he jumped in excitement and said "Master Alex and Master John, how long I have been looking for you. Come with me. The car is this way."

They followed without saying anything. He led them out. Then they saw it. A Limo! Two men came out and took their luggage. The man who picked them up at the airport opened the doors and made them comfortable inside. Soon the Limo took off. Alex wanted to talk to the driver. He found a mike there.

He spoke through it. "Hello, driver. Um, just out of curiosity, where are we going right now?"

He waited and then there it was. He said "Why, sir to the hotel, of course."

And he kept on driving. Alex and John were sightseeing. The driver put a sudden but soft break. They opened the doors and led Alex and John out. They looked out and saw a great and grand entrance of a hotel. Its name was '**OLYMPUS HOTEL**'.

They entered it. There were chandeliers hanging from the ceiling. There were statues of Greek warriors. The hotel was a mix of both modern and old.

They went to the reception. As soon as they came near the reception, one man politely said "Master Alex and Master John, we have been expecting you. Your luggage is already in your suite. Please come with me. I will show you the way."

They followed the man to the fourth floor. He led them into the suite with the name *Dipylone* on the door. He opened it. They were too stunned to move. Inside there was a huge chandelier hanging, a huge balcony, two big bedrooms, both with bathrooms huge as well, a chimney, a big T.V and the whole suite was air conditioned.

They saw their bags were already kept in the bedrooms. The helpers soon left.

First of all they took a nice bath. They also found a dining hall. There was already food kept there. They had their dinner. They opened their bags and found their clothes. To their surprise there were two full body armors too. They decided to try it out.

They put on the chainmail, breast plates, and then the protective things for legs, shoulders and hands. They then put on the helmet and went to look at the mirror. But as they stood opposite the mirror, they saw nothing!! In the mirror there was nothing at all. No Alex, No John. But they could see each other.

That was when it struck John. He said to Alex "Hey, do you know what this means. We are invisible to others. Isn't that great?"

Alex replied "It sure is great but this helmet is pretty heavy."

Suddenly a voice said "Helmet? Did anyone say helmet? If you did, here I am, at your service."

The sound came from both Alex's and John's helmets. They immediately removed it and kept on the table. They both asked "what can you do?"

The helmets replied "We control the armor. We can make you visible or invisible. But we can't predict when we can make you invisible. It is beyond our control and it just happens! We can also make you move as we like."

"How?" Alex asked.

"You want to see? All right. Hey John, have you ever seen your little brother do a ballet. I'm sure you haven't. But look at this."

Suddenly Alex began to move. He stood on one of his toes and was spinning around like professional ballerinas!!!

It looked funny because it was the first time anyone did ballet with body armor!

Soon Alex stopped dancing. Alex said "Never ever do those kinds of thing to me again, understand?"

The helmet replied laughing "All right. I think you guys should probably get to sleep now. We have big things for tomorrow."

They removed the body armor. John had tough time removing it. Then they went to sleep. Their bed was very comfy. So they had a good night's sleep.

CHAPTER SIX

"The Golden Key"

Alex and John, both woke up late the next morning. Alex was the first one up. He found the coffee ready on the table. He also found that his coffee has become cold. He was thinking what to do when he heard a knock. He went and opened it. He found the man at the reception at their door.

He said "Good morning sir, you have a package. Here you go. Thank you, sir."

He gave Alex a small box and left. Alex opened it. He found a small fire extinguisher in it! Then there was also a letter there.

He took out the letter to read it. Nothing was there. But when Alex wished to read, letters started visible in it! It was like this 'Good morning Alex, did you sleep well?

The fire extinguisher is the golden key that will lead to us. Did you see the news? Put on channel 26 and you will see.'

Alex stopped reading and put on the T.V. On channel 26 he saw the news about some shipwreck. They were saying the ship's name was 'SS Titan'.

He thought 'why would the writer of the letter write about some shipwreck.' He thought for some more time. Then it struck him. SS Titan was the name of the ship in which they also planned to travel!!

The man has saved them from the disaster. Alex took the letter and started to read the rest. 'No need to say thanks. We had to keep you alive.'

The letter was almost over 'By the way, I think the coffee should be enough hot by now.'

There was nothing more visible in the piece of paper.

Alex thought 'why did he mention about the coffee?'

He looked at the table. There was no coffee there. He looked around. He could not find it. At last he found it at the least expected place. In the chimney and inside the burning.

He took the fire extinguisher that he received earlier. He dozed the fire. He found the coffee cup there in the middle. He was amazed to find that nothing had happened to the cup. Then he touched the cup slightly to check whether it was hot or not. He found it at the very temperature that he left it at the table!

He found that the coffee was warm enough for him to drink. He remembered the letter. It said that the fire extinguisher was the golden key.

As Alex was thinking about these John also woke up. John asked Alex why there is a fire extinguisher lying on the table. Alex explained everything to him.

He said "I will get refreshed and then we shall discuss about it."

Alex returned to the living room. He thought 'why did the man say 'golden' key, why not any key?'

By then John came. Alex asked John about this. He also began guessing. They thought for ten whole minutes and got nothing. Then John hit the buzzer.

He said to Alex "I think he did not say about that cylinder as golden key. Maybe he said about the golden key that we received when we killed that crab like thing. Don't you remember that voice we heard? It said that this key will lead us to them."

Alex then replied "The idea fits in correctly, but where does this key fit into? Ok, I think I can guess the answer to that. It may fit somewhere near the chimney. Maybe inside it"

They both went and looked inside the chimney. Alex was right. There was a door there. There was the key slot. John brought the key. As he was about to enter the key into it, Alex stopped him and said "Maybe we should go prepared. We should take our swords, wear the armor and take that bottle of tablets. Oh, and the coins too."

"Maybe you're right. Let's go get ready."

Soon they got ready and again came near the chimney. John took the key. He inserted it and turned to look at Alex. Alex nodded in approval. Then he turned the key. They heard a sound coming. Both guessed it was water again. They both said "oh . . . not again."

But this time Alex had an idea. He told John to use ice magic and block the water. Alex and John took their positions. They just put on all their strength. They both closed their eyes and hoped that they will not feel a splash.

Fortunately they didn't. When they opened their eyes, they saw ice in front of them like an arch. When they looked at the chimney, they found that the small door had been destroyed and a wide open space is right in its place.

The water has been frozen so they climbed upon it to see what lay ahead for them. They couldn't see anything.

They took their things and went on walking through the ice. It was very dark in there and they used their torches.

John, while walking, flashed his torch on the ice. He could see beneath the ice. He saw fishes swimming in there.

He called Alex and showed this and said "Alex this means that the layer of ice in which we are walking might be thin. We should eat the tablet and get ready."

Alex took the tablets and ate them and gave one to John. As they took another step they heard a crack. John was right. It was indeed a thin layer of ice. The next step and both of them went tumbling down into the freezing water.

Gladly they could breathe under water. But at the same time it was very cold also. They walked on and on. They saw many fishes swim past them. It was a very long corridor. At last they saw the other end of the long and boring corridor. The other end was also ice. They both took their swords.

Alex said "on your mark, 3 2 1, Goooo."

They smashed down the ice wall. Water gushed out carrying all the fishes with it. Somehow they managed not to be carried by the water. They saw that the water went down instead of going straight. That meant only one thing. The floor has got cracks. Huge cracks.

They both looked down standing on the very edge of the huge crack. They felt like standing at the top of a gigantic cliff. They could merely see the bottom of it which was covered with water.

Alex said "What do we do now?"

John replied "Well, only one thing to do now. Let's go flying."

Saying this John took out the tablets. He gave one to Alex and searched one for himself. Alex was ready but John havent found one yet. After some boring minutes for Alex and some pain taking minutes for John, he at last found one and swallowed it before it went missing.

They both took positions and leapt into darkness. They were flying. But surprisingly not up or straight as they planned! But straight down into cold water and pitch dark and everything else that lay there.

They fell into the water with a huge splash. John and Alex struggled to get out of the water. But something kept pulling them back into the water. They tried on and on but that 'something' kept pulling them back more and deeper into the water. That's when John realized the fact that he can breathe.

He thought 'I guess I accidently took the wrong tablets.' As he was thinking just lying there at the bottom of this new pool that they had created, he saw Alex swimming towards the surface. John was about to go after him when he saw a most shocking sight. One of the sting rays.

The sting ray which had been swimming about all this time came near Alex and one of its two long fins transformed into a long hand. It reached out and grabbed Alex's leg and started to pull him back into the water.

John picked up some stones that were lying there and threw it aiming at the fish. The aim was fine, but the stone did not go far because it was in water. How far can it go, right? So, John searched for something more efficient.

Then he took out his sword and swam towards Alex. As he reached near the fish he struck the sword and cut its hand. Alex became free and looked back to see what had happened. He saw something black dissolving into the water. There was a sting ray swimming around it. The black substance was coming from one of its long fins.

Then he saw that the sting ray moving in a circular manner. It made a small tornado like thing in the middle of the water. The black substance also joined the tornado. It made the whole tornado go black.

Suddenly the sting ray which was swimming around all this time went inside the black substance. As Alex watched, the black substance covered the wide opening through which the fish went in. Then it began to shrink. It shrank and shrank and at last disappeared. It appeared as if a tornado like thing hasn't occurred in that place for years, even a small one.

Then Alex saw John swimming nearby with a sword in his hand. Alex went towards him. Then Alex suddenly realized that he had to go back to breathe in air.

John saw this and swiftly pulled him back into the water and said "Hey, where are you going. We can breathe. I must have accidently switched the tablets. I will tell you what happened earlier . . ."

John explained it all to Alex. How the fish's fin transformed into a long hand and how he stopped it from pulling Alex back. After John stopped explaining Alex said "That must have been another test from them. We must be careful and ready for the next one. I think now we should search around us. There may be some trapdoor hidden somewhere"

John nodded. Suddenly they heard a faint sound. They tried to listen more carefully. It was a voice of someone speaking to someone. Soon the voice became clearer and louder. They could hear what they were speaking about.

"Hey Damen, you ready with your presentation yet? Boss will be busy because he is bringing in two freshmen. Now, what was their name . . . some Alex and John, I think. I heard they got skills in fighting and have good brain."

Damen said "I got plenty of time, my dear Nicholas. After all, before reaching Olympus, they got one more test ahead of them,' the hall of fire'. All I am worried about is them taking my position as team leader in zone 7. But, that will happen only if they survive. As you know, it is not that easy. First they have to find the book of spells. Then they shall have to protect themselves from those silly bats. Then one of them has to read the spell to protect both of them from fire. Those fools will think that there is no reason to worry of fire once they have entered the hall of fire. But the spell only lasts for 10 minutes. I am sure that they will die in the hall of fire and I can remain as team leader"

Nicholas said "Not so fast Damen. I have seen them in action. Also I know their past record which gave me a shocking report, which does not make me accept you as team leader, mate. You know, their father is none other than Sir Blake."

Damen gasped "The sons of Mr. Blake. Well, still I hope this doesn't makes my dreams shattered. Why am I talking about the future? It's already happened. I guess I shall go to my place. If you want me, I will be there."

Alex and John were listening to all this. And promptly they were writing this all down, in their mind.

Alex said "We must find the book of spells. It must be inside a room."

They both searched. They at last found one door. There was something written in it.

They both read it. 'Aqua Destructo'.

They said to each other at the same time "Only water can destroy it?"

They thought how to do that one. They are surrounded by water. There is only one door which needs to be opened and it can only be opened with water.

At last they both came with a solution. Alex said that "we should take all the water from there and shoot it at the door. Then maybe it will break."

They both took control of the water and did what Alex said. The water hit the door like a cannon. But nothing happened! The door stayed as strong as ever.

Then Alex asked John about his idea. John suggested that they should convert the water around the door to ice. Then they should take their swords and strike the ice.

Alex liked the idea very much. They tried it out. The water around the door was made into ice with their ice magic. Then they gathered all the power they had and struck the ice. The ice broke into many smaller pieces and settled down because of the mighty blow that they gave it. They looked at the door. The door didn't break but there was a huge crack in it.

They decided to do it again. They again cooled the water and struck the ice. This time the door was shattered into endless number of pieces. They both went in through that door.

John went first expecting Alex to follow and all the water too. As Alex set his foot on the floor, he felt something warm from his back. He looked back. The water wasn't coming into the room. It was coming but just vanishing before reaching him. Alex went back to see why water was not coming. He saw an astonishing sight. He called John and asked him to come and take a look. John wondered what it was. When he saw it he also found it amazing.

There was a huge hole in that floor through which they just came and through that hole a huge ball of fire with sharp edges was coming. The fire swallowed the water down. Both the brothers were watching it closely and were wondering what's going to happen next. They had a feeling that it will explode any moment and as they guessed it suddenly exploded and covered the whole area with fire.

But luckily John and Alex by that time moved away and were safe. They headed inside just in time or else nobody would even find their carcasses left. Such was the power of the fire. They both were still crouching and hiding their faces from the heat. They waited for some time to see if anything will again happen. But nothing happened.

The fire raged on without any interruption as if it was burning for years. As nothing happened they rose and Alex took the liberty to lead them to the dark mysterious door in which they expected many strange secrets!

CHAPTER SEVEN

"The Book Of Spells"

WITH SWORDS RAISED ALEX went forward to turn the handle and see what evil force lay inside. As Alex touched it a whirling sound came from inside. But that did not stop Alex. He just turned the handle and it opened with a screech.

After a moment as he was about to take his first step into it a gust of wind came out of nowhere and made them fall. They both could get hold of a very disgusting smell. But, with their nose closed, they stepped inside the room.

At one corner of the room they could see blood stains. Alex went near to them. John was observing the rest of the room. On one side he found tiny holes on the wall. He looked at what the holes were pointing at. He found that it was pointing straight at Alex.

He suddenly heard a sound like some gears turning. John soon realized that it was coming from inside the wall. Soon something would come out from there and hit Alex!

John thought of nothing else and made a run for it. Meanwhile Alex was getting closer the corner. He suddenly heard John's voice. He turned and saw that John running towards him and was yelling. Alex couldn't hear anything. The floor was like just going to break with all the stomping from John.

Alex's eye suddenly went to the opposite end of the room. He found arrows coming through small holes at them. Alex didn't know what to do. He just stood there when John came and slammed him down!

Just a millisecond after, many arrows came and struck the wall. As they watched the arrows got pulled in. The wall just swallowed it!!

John moved aside to lie down. But he was sure that something poked at his back very hardly. He screamed loudly. Alex told him to lie face down. Alex saw a huge arrow struck into John's back!! The arrow had pierced his armor and blood was coming out of it.

John asked him what it was that made him scream. When John had heard what Alex had to say, he said "hmm, it's a bit strange because I can't feel any pain. Actually I don't feel anything at all. Let me see if I can move."

He tried to rise. But some invisible force made him lay there. He used all his force, but how much he tried he just couldn't stand up. Alex also tried to pull him up. But John couldn't get up.

"Alex Why don't you find that Book of Spells while I rest in here." John simply said without any fear.

"You sure you'll be alright?"

"Don't worry about me. I'll be alright."

Alex put the tablets, the scroll, everything except Roark and stood up and walked straight leaving behind the wounded John.

Alex searched for some clues or something. As he walked he suddenly saw many doors straight ahead of him. He didn't know which one to go through. He looked at each door. Each of it had some kind of picture embedded on them. Alex looked closely. It was pictures of animals. There was a bull, a bat, a fox and a dove.

Alex remembered about the talk they heard in the water. '**Then they have to escape from those stupid bats**'.

So Alex thought it would be best for him to go through the door with the symbol of bats. He drew Roark and opened the door with courage. Alex thought 'that man said stupid bats. So I guess it will be easy for me.'

The door opened like flowing water. He went in. It was dark. Alex noticed that there was a glow coming from his body. He slowly took his first step. As he lifted his leg for the next step, something sticky fell from nowhere and covered his body! He couldn't see anything.

Alex then felt the sticky mess getting harder. He acted quickly. He made his sword move here and there. He tried to jump. At last he found a small opening. He widened it by using his hands. It was wide enough for a man to squish out. He struggled and finally got out.

He looked around him. There was light everywhere. The sticky mess had become hard like concrete!! Alex saw straight ahead of him the book of spells floating by some magic on a pedestal!!

There was also a light surrounding the book. Alex went straight for it. He looked around. There was nobody about. He raised his hands and swiftly took it. He thought something would happen. But there was nothing.

But, all of a sudden there was a sound. The light which was surrounding the book became faint and Alex could hear a weak sound of something rattling above him. He understood what it was. He started to make a dash to the door through which he came in.

He had not even reached half of the distance when a swarm of bats flew in to the room through a small opening. They were catching up very quickly. When the bats reached just above Alex, they began to descend down on him. They started to peck him at his back. But the armor protected him from harm.

He finally reached the door and closed it as soon as he got past the door. He could hear the bats hitting the door and falling down!!

Alex ran to John. John was not lying anymore! Alex ran to him with the book of spells in his hands. John then asked Alex "I think when you got the book in your hand; I could stand up to my wish. Looks like you had a tough time."

Alex opened it. First a flash came from the pages and slowly it blurred and Alex further leaned forward to read it. It was in ancient Greek. Alex knew that he couldn't read it but he still concentrated on the page. For his astonishment the Greek letters slowly turned into English!!

He could easily read it. The title read 'spell for antitoxin to any toxic substance. The other page read 'spell to make you the most beautiful person in the world'. Alex flipped the pages and saw 'spell for a protective safeguard all around the body for 2 hours'

"John, I think this would be an appropriate choice."

"Yeah I guess." Alex read the spell.

It was just some rubbish. As he read it a white thing started to cover Alex and John from the legs to the top. Then they took their things and waited for the safeguard to cover their whole body. As soon as it covered them from head to toe they started to the door and out to the hall of fire, wherever it was.

But the ball of fire was still there. And was much bigger by then. Alex went near and tried to touch it. He did but nothing happened to him! He jumped into the fire. To his amazement, he found himself floating!

John too jumped in and said "you had me scared there buddy."

They both then started off to a wall which was just near there. Alex's opinion was that one should search from the top and the other from the bottom of the wall. John said he would go to the bottom and so Alex went to the top. They kept searching frantically for a few minutes and when reached the centre they both saw a very bright light on the opposite side brighter than the orb of blaze.

They were both pulled to it by some strange magic. As Alex was just about to go towards it, a voice said to him 'Don't do it Alex. It will only lead you to your death. Pull back your brother. You are making a mistake'

Alex came to his senses. He saw John just beside him. He was going near it. Alex just used all his energy and pushed him aside. John also came to his wits. Alex told him what had happened. They both rose and looked at the place from where the light was coming from.

The light had by then dimmed off. In its place was a small cavity. One could hardly squish through it. John insisted that he went first. Alex made way for him. He drew his sword and went through it. As John's legs disappeared into the darkness Alex shouted through the hole "hey are you there? Are you fine?"

"Yes, I am. Wait a minute. The tunnel is coming to an end."

There was a pause. Alex waited eagerly for John to say something.

"Alex, you won't believe this. Do come over" it was time for Alex to make his move.

He too squeezed through it. The tunnel was a bit long. But he managed it. After the tunnel was a huge hall, where Alex saw John waiting for him. Alex also came in to the huge hall. John was standing just beside him. "Why did you call me? What is here, John?"

"Look around for yourself"

Alex turned to look all round the hall. He noticed that the long and tall hall was fully embedded with sparkling diamonds!! They were on the floor too. He was about to pick one up when John stopped him.

"Let's not be hasty, brother."

"You're right. It might be a trap."

When Alex stood up he struck a piece of diamond and it came off from its place. Suddenly the place started rumbling as if a massive earthquake had struck it.

"I think we should fly, John" and Alex took himself out of the ground.

John also flew up to Alex. Alex pointed his fingers at the top of the corridor. There a small door emerged from the roof. They flew to it. Just then pieces of diamonds started falling from the ceiling. They dodged it swiftly. Still one of them hit Alex. But thanks to his armor nothing serious happened to him.

They soon reached at the door. The door easily opened and they went through it. The inside was full of darkness. Alex felt around the wall. After some time he could find out a lever. He put it on. Nothing happened. Then all of a sudden lights started shimmering.

There was only light in the entire area. They could see what was going on. They couldn't believe their eyes. They were then standing in the middle of a city. The door through which they just came in here became the door of a house!

CHAPTER EIGHT

"The Ancient Village"

J OHN AND ALEX LOOKED around. There was just one problem. The village was of medieval time!

Old fashioned houses, people wearing long robes, people selling bread, meat and vegetables openly without any cover in small shops. They guessed where they were. In the middle of an ancient Greek city!

Alex went to a woman nearby. He wanted to ask her where they were in English. But when he did so, it came out of his mouth in ancient Greek! John who was standing near a street light noticed that the people didn't even mind them. They just walked past them without even noticing them. John wondered why?

Then he saw his brother and thought that he was a fool to ask a complete stranger who doesn't even speak their language. But when he heard Alex speak Greek his mouth fell open in astonishment.

But in response, the lady looked at Alex for a few seconds and stood aside and shrieked at the top of her voice. Suddenly soldiers with spears rushed into the scene. The folks of the city also gathered around her.

John was afraid that he and Alex would be caught for scaring the poor lady. He also moved in on to Alex. When everybody had assembled, the old lady said "a ghost talked to me." Though she did talk in Greek, Alex and John understood each word as if they were listening it in English!

A voice then came from amidst the people "What exactly happened?"

"As I was picking up flowers, I heard someone asking me something. I turned back to answer him but there was no one to be seen. I looked around for but no, there was nobody."

Alex thought he was just a fraction of second away from getting a nice beating but when he heard the woman talking rubbish, he sighed in relief. He signaled John to go and stand behind a house and that he would meet him there.

Alex then moved more closer to the people. He then just howled, like a wolf does in twilight. That much was enough for the villagers to have a shiver down their spine and to run frantically for a shelter!!

The old woman gushed into the house just behind her. The soldiers vanished just like they first appeared, out of nowhere. From some places, John and Alex could hear sound of pots breaking, metals clinging and some injuries too.

In the midst of this chaos, Alex carefully avoiding the people made his way to John. "Why do you think the woman didn't see me?"

"It's because you are wearing the armor which makes you invisible fool. You noticed one more thing? Though they speak in their language, somehow we are able to understand the same. Don't you?

"Alright. But where do we go now?"

"While you were scaring the people off, I noticed the soldiers going over that direction."

"To the forest?"

"Yes Alex, to the forest."

"But what use is that to us following the soldiers?"

"You know, the soldiers will always lead us right to their chief. Maybe he will be able to tell us what's going on."

"But don't you think we probably should stop by to take a break."

"Alright. Let me ask for some water."

John removed his helmet, breastplate and soon all his armor. He was visible then. He came out from the back of the house. He straight went to a youngster. "Hey boy, can I get some water?"

"You bet. Just wait here. I'll be back in a minute."

He then ran off to a house nearby and then vanished in to the darkness.

John thought 'the children of this time are better than those in their own time.' He recalled one incident when he once asked a small boy for a little water. The kid kicked his leg and ran away.

Alex couldn't bear it any more. He slowly moved without making any noise. He slowly whispered to John "John, where is the water? I couldn't wait there anymore."

"Just keep your mouth shut. The water will be along any minute."

The boy then came running along with a lady. She had a pot in her hand. She said "he told me that a man was standing alone in front of our small hut and asked for water. We have a well just in the back. So I just pulled out some and emptied them into the pot here."

She handed the pot to John. "Would it hurt you if you just bring one more pot? My brother, he's rather shy. He is just behind that house."

"Yeah, sure. Just wait here." Again the lady and the kid went in to the house.

John drank the water. Just when he was about to finish, Alex tipped off the pot. John was just about to get it, but it got out of his hands. The noise made the town folk to look at John "Sorry, a bit clumsy. Please get on with your work."

"Shy, huh, brother."

"You had a better idea, then." Alex remained silent.

"Thought so" said John.

The lady then came back. The kid was inside. She looked at the broken pieces of her pot. "What happened?"

"Pot got slipped from my hands. I'm very sorry."

"That's okay, here's water for your brother."

John went to the back of the house. Alex took the pot away from John and began to drink down all of it. John gave the pot back to the lady.

He came back, put his armor on and they made their way into the forest, following the soldiers.

A little in, they could smell roasted meat of some animal. They began to follow the smell and finally found the place. The soldiers were camping in a small clearing. The smell was coming from there. They were cooking deer meat.

One of them said "I wish our chief could just stop giving orders, you know."

"Yeah. All he does is enjoy in his small palace in the village. All because of us."

This information was enough for Alex and John. They started on their way back. By then it was evening.

Everything in the village was slowly getting closed. They had to find a decent place to stay for the night. They took their armors off. The inns were full and most of the residents didn't let them sleep in their houses. They thought it would be best if they asked the same lady from whom they took water to let them stay for the night.

They knocked at the wooden door. It was the child who opened the door. Before anyone could say anything, the child ran back inside with the same speed he came to open the door. Then the lady came up.

"Oh, this is the shy brother you told me about."

John gave a hit to Alex. "Yeah"

"Come in now both of you."

The house was nice and clean and big. It was made of clay bricks and was cool inside. The floor was tiled. There was a portrayal of Zeus hung on the wall. He was standing on a huge cloud with a lightning sparkling with unlimited power and ready to annihilate anything that stands in its way. He was looking very grand in that posture.

It also had a first floor. The bedrooms were all there overlooking to a central courtyard. They noticed that, in the kitchen, they cook with firewood. There were sacks full of grains also.

Alex and John stayed in the main hall. There was a statue of a man just adjacent to the portrait of Zeus. The lady then came back with bread and fruits on a plate.

"Take a seat."

They sat down on two small stools. She laid the plate on the minor table.

"Go on."

Alex leaned to take an apple. But John rushed and took a slice of bread. There was only one slice of bread but many pieces of apple.

"I am very sorry. That's all what's left"

"We wanted to ask you that will you let us stay here for tonight."

"Well, you are strangers to this place but you seem nice, so yes."

"We are very thankful for you to show this kind of kindness to complete strangers." said Alex.

"But one thing very strange about you that I find is your clothes. I have never seen any type of clothes like these. You are not from around here, are you?"

"Not quite."

"In your clothes, you two are real strangers. I will also get some cloths for you by the morning. You can't go out in this."

She led them upstairs. There was a room vacant. The other two were for the child and the lady.

The room was a bit cranked but it was okay. She left them and soon the lights came down. They lay down in the bed placing their bags and things below the bed. They were exhausted after that day's adventure. But something was keeping them feel that this was just the beginning only.

It was a bird's sweet sound and sun's warmth that made the brothers rise up to their feet. They took a moment to understand where they were. It all came back to them. At a small table near the bed, there were two shirts with a bottom open like a skirt and two long pieces of cloth.

Wearing the shirt was not a problem. But the cloth, they had to do it a dozen and at last got right. Then they looked just like two Roman citizens!

They went down the stairs. And out of the house. The village was already moving quickly. Everybody was doing their daily chores. They went round the house. The lady was their doing some laundry work.

When she saw them, she smiled and said "it suits you both well."

"I only have one question in my mind, isn't this supposed to be a Greek village?" John asked.

"Yes" replied the lady.

"Then why are we wearing the Roman clothes?"

She giggled "You two absolutely have no sense. But I can now understand that you are coming here for the first time. The Romans and the Greeks wear almost the same dress. I also have to tell you one more thing."

She lowered her voice "Lately the Romans have seized the Greek. They want us to follow their ways."

Looking at them she said "You haven't bathed, have you? You should go to the *thermae* situated just near here" Though a new word, Alex guessed it to be a bath house.

Pointing to the small road she said "You take a right after this *insulae* and then the second left from there. After bathing you go to the *popinae* and buy something for yourself. Do you have any money with you?"

From her actions and directions, John and Alex thought, they were learning new words very fast!! Whatever knowledge John had on Greek also helped. John told Alex "Popinae means cheap eating place, OK?"

"Yeah, that we have." John replied to the lady.

"Meanwhile I have to go to the *polis* and pray in the temple of Athena on top of the *acropolis* and buy little something from the *agora*. I just hope I don't pop up in front of the *oligarch* who is running the polis. One nasty fellow he is"

It was too fast for Alex to learn and he looked at John. As if he knew every word of Greek, John explained to Alex "Polis means Greek city and Agora is a market place. Acropolis seems a small hill."

"And *Oligarch?*" asked Alex.

"I think the city head, only a guess." John replied.

Saying these to them she went in. John and Alex took some Drachmas with them and concealed it safely in their dress. They went straight as she said. Then took a right. Then the second left and there it was. ***Thermae***, the bath house!

The entrance was wide and above the ground. They climbed the steps. There were pillars that looked like that of Roman architecture. They went in. A man was sitting in a table with a register in his hands. Folks came out of a chamber and paid the man and went out. He jotted down quickly who came and how much they paid.

Alex and John went near him.

The man said "Are you going to just stand there or say something."

They went near him. "So, bath or steam?" he asked.

"Bath" both of them said at the same time.

"Alright. Keep your clothes there and enjoy."

He pointed his finger opposite. There was a door and it was covered with curtains. They slowly walked towards it as if it was a ferocious dragon and was going to eat them any second!!

They went in, put their gowns at a small corner and entered a large tub. There were others also. They were chatting, relaxing. They felt that this was like their meeting place. Alex and John also joined them in that tub.

The water was a bit cold but nice. It was really refreshing after their tiring journey yesterday. They closed their eyes for some time and relaxed. After some time when they opened their eyes there was silence everywhere. There was no one in the bath. The whole place felt dead!

They looked around. In the opposite corner of the tub there was a small figure. But unlike them he was wearing the dress and still was not wet!!

He smiled at them and began to swim towards them.

He said "Hi. You both have passed the test. Roark, Nemesis, you two have also done a good job."

Two blades came sprouting from nowhere near Alex and John.

"Always a pleasure" said Roark.

The stranger turned back to Alex and John. "It's time."

John said "Time for what? Who are you?"

He grinned at that and raised his hands. Water rose from around him. It covered all of them and then they simply vanished.

CHAPTER NINE

"The God's Mission"

WHEN JOHN OPENED HIS eyes he was lying down in a bed. His eyes were hurting. Alex was also lying next to him. He stood up and looked around. Roark and Nemesis were lying there.

There was a window. He looked out of it. There were clouds. When he looked down, he gasped. He was standing on top of a tall building. All he could see was clouds and clouds!!

There were some birds flying way down. He went and woke up Alex. It took him a minute to understand where he was or how he got there. He too looked out of the window. Suddenly he saw a plane coming straight at them. He showed it to John. They didn't know what to do. There wasn't any door in the room. The plane kept advancing straight on them. They couldn't do anything.

They took their swords and got ready. But the plane did not crash when it came; it just came through the building as if it was made of air! It even went through them too but just as they were inside the plane, it turned real again!! They then realized that it passed through the building making them inside the plane. They were flying in the plane, direct from their room!! They couldn't believe boarding a plane like this.

Alex could tell John that they were in a private jet, as this plane just had only 6 to 8 seats. He also noticed a mini bar. There were two people standing near the door which led to the pilot's cabin.

Suddenly the men came near them and said "please have your seats."

Those two men led them to two nearby seats. At their opposite was a young man wearing suits and all, with a look of a business man.

He said "Hi. Have some food. I know that you both are hungry. I hope the tests we have been giving you have been fun and interesting."

The man waved his hands. The table became laden with all kinds of food.

Alex was thinking 'fun, interesting, is he insane. We nearly died in most of their so called 'tests'.

Suddenly the man said "We had to be sure."

Alex turned to him and understood that he read his mind. He smiled when Alex thought of that. He grinned back. Putting an end to their silent conversation John asked the man "That we can fight?"

"No, that you were the true sons of Blake."

Alex made his first move for the food. He took two apples in his hands. John took some sandwiches. It felt like the sweetest thing they have ever tasted.

The man then said "Now to business. First let's put you up to speed. I am Zeus, God of the sky, weather, thunder, lightning, law, order, and fate. I am the son of Cronus and Rhea and I . . . ."

"And I . . . what?" asked Alex

"And I was the king of Gods at Olympus."

"What do you mean *was*?"

"I will tell you that later."

A question arose in John's mind "How are you still this young?" he asked.

"Hey kid, five hundred million years is like a day to me. Besides I can shape-shift too."

Being called a kid sounded a little strange to them at first. Zeus then said "Cronus, my father is now ruling the world. Please do not get misguided that he is ruling *your* world. There are many worlds. The Greek settlement you saw is one of them. So is yours. Please understand that there are worlds more advanced than yours."

He snapped his hands. The food on the table disappeared. Zeus said "I will just make you believe that there are some more advanced worlds than yours"

A screen appeared on the table. In it they saw people flying rather in vehicles to get somewhere. Some of them were getting into a small room and then pressed some button which teleported them to anywhere they wanted.

He said "Just to relax you, Do you want to see how the future ninjas sneak into a building?"

"Yes"

On the screen the visual changed and they saw four ninjas. They took out four cloaks. One for each. Then they said something to each other and put on their cloak. The second they put it on they became invisible!

He snapped his fingers again. The screen went through the table as if it were not there.

"Aren't those ninjas wonderful? Now what was I saying?"

"About Cronus ruling the world . . ."

"Yes right. Everyone in your world believes that Zeus is ruling the world. But do you know the truth? Do you want to know more?"

"Oh, we would very much be obliged."

"Cronus is still ruling the world" he stopped for a while.

"The battlefield was your earth. All of earth stood watching the battle. At the battle that decided it all, we were winning. And all the titan lords down our feet. Even Cronus himself was down. In order to put them to pieces and throw them into Tartarus, the underworld zone of eternal torment, I took Cronus's scythe. I gave one blow to his chest but he stayed intact. So I put all the humans to sleep to take their power too." Zeus stopped again for a while.

"Then something unexpected happened. The power of all the humans in the earth, instead of coming to me went straight to the scythe!" he again stopped for a moment.

"While I was figuring out what to do, Cronus somehow rose to his feet and knocked me down! My victory was short lived!! My brothers and sisters could only watch. Before I could come back to my senses, he took his scythe from me. With all the human power behind, he began to gain more power. His brothers, the titan lords, also rose. As I said my victory was short lived and we were beaten. That is it." Zeus again stopped.

"That's it? After giving enough confusion, you mean it?"

"Yeah that's it. Anyway, now we have more important things to discuss, don't you think?"

"Yeah sure go on."

"So Cronus is now ruling. We need to regain our world. Once we had an oracle which said Mr Blake from earth will come and help us to fight with Cronus. It said Mr Blake will have a plan and powers to make us win over

Cronus. But Mr Blake's effort could not be completed. That's a big story which you will know later. As I said earlier we need to take over the lost power from Cronus. For that first you have to take over his brothers. We were about to start off with Oceanus, the powerful titan of Cronus, but we didn't know his location. That's when we heard about you. The oracle said that two sons of Sir Blake shall come forth and put an end to everything. It also said, there will be obstacles, but ultimately we will be the winners."

He continued "Please remember. The oracle also said that **"they shall still be betrayed by a friend that they have had use of so much"**. Poseidon, my brother, was very thrilled by the news of you two that he himself went to see that you two were tested properly and that you reached here safely. Hades, my other brother also did a little part getting you ahead in time, alright?"

"Alright"

"Since you left your world, Poseidon sensed something in the ocean in your world and guessed it was Oceanus and headed out. But suddenly Poseidon also disappeared. We sent people to search him but there was no word of him. First of all you two are going to find him. But before that you need further training."

"Training? Where?"

"Here" He pointed out.

Alex and John looked out. They had landed. There was a nice and big cottage with farmlands and vast areas of plain grass.

"This is where you will be living and training till we say you are ready."

"Okay, no problem but where are we?"

"You are in another world. It's the only safe place that we've still got. That's all you need to know right now."

People came from the cottage. They were dressed in old fashioned way. They went to the back of the plane and came back with the bags of Alex and John that they had brought to the hotel in Greece. They also brought some other bags too. Alex could hear metals clashing on to each other. For the first time in a few days, Alex and John did not feel surprised.

"I hope the information given is sufficient. More will be given form inside. I suggest you now close your eyes."

They both closed their eyes. They felt a flicker.

When they opened their eyes Zeus was gone and so was his plane.

Chapter Ten

"The Arena"

Alex and John understood that Zeus has left and had made them aware about their mission. They have to find out Poseidon.

They glanced upon the cottage where they were left. They could see the last of the men taking their bags inside. Roark who was silent for the entire time in their waist woke up.

"Ah there is nothing like the smell of fresh air and green grass".

Alex said "Let's go check out the cottage"

They went running up to the cottage. There were also some small huts nearby the cottage. It looked almost like a small village. They went in to the cottage. The roof of the cottage was covered with hay. It was very comfy inside. There was a main hall with a door on one corner. There was a chandelier hanging. Alex spotted the door in a corner. He went near it while John was taking a glance at the big portrait on the wall.

On the door it was written "Door of wishes." Near the door there was a circular board like a roulette which was divided into many parts with lines. Things were written on these parts. There was also a pointer and a button at the middle.

When Alex looked closer, he understood that it was names of Gods written on these parts. He called down John. When they tried to open the door, it was locked. John had some idea in mind and turned the pointer to Ares, the God of war. Then Alex pressed the button in the middle.

There was a sudden sound of gears turning all around the house. It made them feel that the house hadn't been touched for years. Then they heard a sound at the door. The door opened with a creak.

When they looked inside they saw a big hall filled with all types of fighting material. Short sword, long sword, one handed sword, two handed sword, spear, javelin, hammer, axe and many more. You name it, it's here. Further, the floor, ceiling and the walls were fully painted in red.

Then suddenly a sound came. "Welcome to Ares' room. Now that you have seen all the weapons armour, etc., I suggest that you walk forward and enter the arena. You may pick your weapon of choice. But I warn you, if you're tired when you enter, oh boys you are sure to die."

The voice died. Alex and John were not hungry. They had some food in the plane. They were not tired either. Their invisibility armour was kept there. They put it on. They took their swords, grabbed some shields, took two spears and walked straight.

They found a door with a label on it named "Arena". When they opened it a light flashed on them for a few seconds making it impossible for them to see what is inside for that few seconds. After the lights cleared out and when they looked out, they couldn't believe their eyes. It was an arena with people cheering.

In the middle there was a giant standing in chains. They walked to the middle. People were shouting like anything. When they reached the middle a ball flew in. It didn't fall down. Instead it flew straight to them. While floating in the air it said to them

"Challengers are you ready?"

"When did we become challengers." said Alex.

"Alright. Thank you. Audience, are you ready?"

"Of course" roared the audience.

Another ball flew right past the Giant and asked "Giant, are you ready?"

A huge roar came from its mouth. It then shaked the chains and its bad breath reached Alex's and John's face.

"I'll take that as a yes. Challengers take your places. We are about to begin."

The ball then went to the top of the arena.

Alex and John took a few steps back. The door from which they came disappeared. A huge speaker then appeared in the middle and said "3 2 1 Go." and it exploded into many tiny little pieces.

The giant's chain broke off. A huge club appeared at the hands of the Giant. Suddenly the invisibility armour paid off at the right moment. The giant couldn't see Alex and John. But it could still see their weapons. They were standing nearby each other. Then they split up when the Giant landed its first blow.

Then something extraordinary happened. Alex and John were standing at opposite ends of the arena. The giant was standing in the middle. Suddenly the giant's two eyes began to move from its position. One of them turned towards Alex and other towards John! After that its hands and legs also did the same. Two new hands and legs emerged from the middle of the body. Then one more head came. Then the giants went away from each other so that they split themselves into two!

After doing so each charged against Alex and John. In fact they turned towards the weapons, knowing that the challengers will be with the weapons! Alex and John noticed that the Giants have become smaller than when they were a whole. Before they could think of anything, the giants picked them up. Then they came to the middle and flung them straight up into air. It felt to Alex and John as if they were going up in slow motion. The ball appeared there very quickly.

It said to them "what you're thinking is right but at the same time wrong too. It happened to give you people time to adjust your position. When you get down, it won't be a slow motion and you will get the same feeling as when you fall down normally"

The ball went back as quick as it came. Alex said "I have an idea."

"I just hope that it's not something crazy. I know that look." said John looking at his face.

"Oh it's crazy alright. First we use our ice magic and make slides. Then at the bottom of the slide we will make a ramp. So we slide and shoot like a jet through the ramp and we will kill the giants. We have to split since we are attacking two giants."

"You sure?"

"Pretty sure. We have a limited window here. Let's go."

Alex said this and put his sword in its sheath and started making the slide from the bottom with the ice magic. John began to do the same. Soon the ice was about to reach them in a few seconds. They took their swords and said good luck to each other.

John said to his helmet "If anything happens to us do something like getting out or killing the giants, alright?"

"Sure thing boss."

The moment the ice touched their legs the slow motion withdrew and they went down fast. From the audience's point of view one second the weapons were going down and the next second they were flying toward the giants. The giants were all this time watching with amazement as two slides and ramps appeared out of nowhere. Then two weapons and invisible men appeared and flew straight at them. Alex used his sword to cut one giant's hands off. John cut down his giant's legs.

Both the giants roared with pain and said "Enough. We accept defeat. You win."

The ball appeared there and said "Challengers win. Do you wish to continue?"

"Um . . . no." They made themselves visible and people could see them wearing normal clothes.

"We look forward for your next meeting."

Another door soon appeared at one end of the arena. Alex and John went through it. It led straight to the kitchen and once they entered that door also vanished. They suddenly realized that they were hungry. There was food laid down on a table. They helped themselves. After a hearty meal they found a new door appearing at one end of the room and they went through it. It led them to the bedroom. Two big beds were there. They lay down on the bed. It was very comfy. Before they could say a word they found themselves sleeping.

They woke up the next morning when sun's first rays reached their face. They found the bathrooms and got fresh. The only door in the room again led them to the kitchen. There a light breakfast was laid out. It was a good one. They returned to the main hall. They sat down for some time. Just then Alex felt he had heard a sound.

He asked John "Did you hear a sound?"

"No"

Then they both heard a small sound. Before they could do anything men came from all parts of the house. They almost gave the two a heart attack. Things happened so quickly that at the blink of an eye they had their swords pointed at their throats and their hands were tied.

Regaining his cool, John murmured to Alex "I have a plan. Just wait and see."

The men were all dressed like one of those Robin Hood's John had seen in movies. More surprisingly they all had the same face. A man emerged from them.

He said "At ease my dear friends. Let them breathe"

All the Robin Hoods put their swords down but were alert and prepared to fight any moment.

The man asked "Who are you and what is it that you want from me?"

Alex tried to provoke him "You the boss? You don't look like one."

He said with a grin "Your cheap tricks won't work on me. Now I will ask one more time, who are you and what are you doing in my house?"

Alex tried another trick "We are the sons of Sir Blake."

"You sure? You sure don't have his skills. Let's hear your names then."

Just then a sound came. All the men turned their faces towards the door of wishes. The door opened slowly. Roark and Nemesis jumped in through the door. The men were taken aback for a second. They soon took their positions. Roark and nemesis went to their masters and cut their bonds.

"You wanted to know our names right. Alex and John" said John.

They took the swords in their hands and began to fight. Even though they were outnumbered badly they fought bravely. Many fell. Alex had a cut on his knee. All this time the boss was simply standing there doing nothing as his men fell one by one.

Soon all the men were down licking the carpet.

The boss then said "You have proved that you really are the sons of Sir Blake. I am Captain Adrian. I serve under **Artemis**, Goddess of the hunt, wilderness, animals, young girls, childbirth and plague. Once I have fought with your father. He was a great man. Zeus told me that you would be coming. But I had to be sure."

"Let me ask you one thing. Why are all your men looking the same and why did you let them down." asked Alex.

Adrian pulled the sleeve of his right hand to reveal a watch like bracelet. It was not much of a watch. There was no dial or anything. Just two switches on its side. "Like I said I had to be sure."

He then pressed one of the buttons. Suddenly all the men disappeared.

"What are they?" asked John.

"They are *Pholograms*. They have the faces of the owner. They don't fight that much but they are great distraction tools."

"So why are you here?" asked Alex.

"To train you." said Adrian.

Alex knew, not to ask why the training.

"Alright when shall we start?"

"Tomorrow as the dew falls on the leaves."

That day they did some skirmishing. They took a stroll on the farm. Then they crashed on the bed.

CHAPTER ELEVEN

"The Training"

THEY SLEPT FOR LONG and hoped the next day should be interesting with Adrian's training plan.

While Alex and John were sleeping, Adrian woke up and had a bath. Then he took a whistle and blew it so hard that Alex and John fell from their beds.

"It's morning. Let's go for training." Adrian said.

They wearily went out of the cottage.

"First, jogging" their coach said.

They started jogging. Alex was still feeling very sleepy. Suddenly he felt a shock on his back. His coach said "There will be punishment if you jog lazily."

After that they began to jog properly. After an hour of continuous jogging they came back to the cottage. Inside they found their coach sitting on a chair. He had them fooled by a Phologram!

He told them "Your father would have noticed. Now you have two minutes to rest, thirty seconds to put on the armor and five seconds to show up in the arena."

"What do you mean? I mean we can't do this" said Alex.

Adrian started moving towards the door. "Ten seconds are over of your two minutes. Please don't be late." he opened it and just disappeared.

There were two bottles kept on a table. Alex and John reached for them. On the label of the bottle it was written 'Energy for tired men. A spoonful and you become a new man.'

There wasn't any spoon around there. So they opened the bottles and slowly put some of that powder into their mouths. They put down the bottles and lay down on the couch. After a few seconds they started to feel as "something" coming to their body. In a few seconds the two who were panting and down on the couch were up and fresh like a new leaf!

They raced to the door. This time they didn't mind to turn the circular piece of board. They went straight in. It was the right place. The long red hall. They put on their armors, grabbed their swords and ran for the arena. When they reached there, Adrian was there ready and a suit of armor was covering his body. It was silver in color. He had a piece of small stick which looked like a sword's handle. On the other hand he had something like a stop watch.

He said, looking at it "You're late. One more thing. Do you always have the habit of taking thing and having it without thinking at least for a few second?"

"Sorry, alright?" said Alex.

"OK, alright. Take positions." He then went back.

He then took the stick and held it up high. Suddenly it became a long sword!

Not waiting to see the beauty of the sword they took their own or they would have known the pain of it too because Adrian had already made a move towards them.

"Be alert always. Don't be distracted."

His sword would have sliced Alex's face if not for his sword. Suddenly Adrian hit his sword at Alex's leg and he fell down.

"Be alert."

John grabbed this opportunity and put his sword at Adrian's neckline. Adrian put a grin on his face and turned around with extreme speed that John's sword fell down. Before Adrian could do anything Alex who was down on the ground, thanks to Adrian, kicked his legs and Adrian fell down. Before he could recover and fight again, Alex got up and took Roark and pushed aside Adrian's and said "Who's distracted now?"

John also joined Alex. The armors then said "Nice moves boss."

Adrian said "Good, that was pretty well for starters, but . . ." he raised his hand.

The sword appeared at his hands. In a flash of second Alex and John were down on their and their swords on Adrian's hands.

"You can never defeat me." He finished his sentence.

They then stood up and took their swords. John asked "Hey Adrian how can you see us when we were told that this is an invisible armor?"

"It's because we are on the same team. Do you remember a few days ago that the giant could not see you? Why? Because it was our enemy."

"Alright, thanks for the info."

"Wait a minute. How do you know of the giants? You weren't even there at that time." Alex asked suddenly

"I was observing you for a very long time. Since your father disappeared."

"Since our father "disappeared"?" asked both of them.

"Surprised? Oh yes . . . for you he is dead. I forgot. Please understand. He didn't actually die that day. He was about to unsheathe a plot to finish the Gods once and for all by Cronus. The archaeologist friend of your father was me only. The diamond you took was a part of it, Alex. Your father had to leave earth to complete his plan."

"But I lost the diamond." Alex said.

"We took it from you. It was sealed away until it was stolen the day Poseidon disappeared."

"What about this necklace?" Alex asked.

"We still don't know what it really does. I found it one day at my doorstep with a note that "Give it to a child who saves your life". So I gave it to you, the one who saved my life. Now let's move on with our training. What is your element? This will be a question frequently asked in the coming days. So what will you say to them?"

Alex said "I think ice is the one for both of us."

Adrian said "No that's your secondary element only. Your primary elements are fire, water, earth and air. Ice is part of water. Did you get your ice power by killing a Majin?"

"Yes" said John.

"I should have known. You should consider yourselves lucky. People hardly get their power from Majins. They are hard to kill. Almost all the people we have called to come here have been tested with a Majin first. Most of them failed their test. Very few people like you have passed the test. All the rest got their powers from ice crystals."

"What's so special about power from Majin?"

"Well it's more powerful and if you have the water as your primary element you can make the ice into water. There are some situations where you can't use your primary element. You have to rely on your secondary element."

86

"Where do we get our primary element from?"

"They are with you from the moment you were born. You have to bring it out yourself. They are randomly placed on some people all over your world and many other worlds too. We can read your body with our power and can understand if you are carrying an element or not."

"What is your element?"

"Mine? You sure you want to know?"

"Yep."

"Then step back."

Suddenly the earth started to shake. Some parts of the arena fell down. Huge chunks of rock started to fall.

"Don't go near the middle." Adrian said to them.

They were already running to the edge of the arena. The center of the arena started to rise. Beneath a layer of sand and rock, metal started to appear. After a few moments a small house appeared there.

"Now watch" said Adrian.

Adrian drew his sword. He raised it up high in the air. Dark clouds began to gather around the arena. Suddenly a jolt of lightning hit the house. It started to melt because of the massive lightning.

Surprisingly Alex or John did not feel its heat. In just a matter of seconds a pile of rubble was seen at the centre of the arena.

"I thought you said there is no such element as lightning."

"Indeed there is no element as lightning. But this is a gift from Zeus. I believe it time for us to end our lessons for today."

They put their weapons and armor in place. When they opened the windows for some fresh air to get in they found that it was night outside.

"What is this?"

"Time moves very quickly in this planet. It's time for you to have your dinner and sleep."

After a hearty meal, they parted to their rooms.

As Adrian was about to sleep two bright faced gentlemen came to his room.

"What do you want?"

"I . . . we came to ask you about one thing."

"And what would that be?" asked Adrian to a confused Alex and John.

"I am sure that there is no creature named Majin in Greek mythology or any other mythology."

"Well there is now."

"How did it come?"

"Well just take it like this. Zeus must have told you that Cronus has put a . . ."

"Yes he told us that."

"Well he also made some creatures that have never been heard in the 'real' world. Do you know the great sea serpent Jormungand? It was killed by Cronus at the great war."

"Wait a minute. The serpent attacked for the gods? I thought it fought against the gods."

"Listen, your knowledge in history won't work here. Whatever you've ever studied about Gods and Goddesses, things work the exact opposite here. Now where was I? Yes the Jormungand was cut into many pieces. It was after the battle that we came to know the pieces gained life. The pieces that fell into the water became aquatic creatures, and the others which fell into the land became horrifying creatures that we now use for battle against Cronus".

"So where does Cronus and his people live?"

"In Muspellheim and Niflheim."

"The underworlds? Why?"

"Believe me son, they are not underworlds anymore.

"So Cronus made us believe that the Gods killed him and now he wants to kill the Gods. Why?"

Adrian yawned "That I will tell to you tomorrow. Find your way out. Good Night."

Adrian closed the door behind them. Alex and John quickly went to their beds. While they were fast asleep in their rooms, Adrian on the other hand was talking to a dark hooded figure.

"What should I tell them tomorrow?"

"Is this why you summoned me in this night. Tell them what I told you. Take them to him as soon as possible."

"Alright." He turned towards his bed.

"But . . ." when he turned all he could see was the moon smiling upon him. Thinking about tomorrow he went to sleep.

CHAPTER TWELVE

"The Jorumnian"

T HE NEXT DAY THE climate was pleasant. Adrian hurried them to the hall. "Go put your armor and come back here".

Imagining what Adrian will be up to they went and put on their armor. When they came back with Roark and Nemesis there was nobody in the hall. Not even a soul to be seen there. They searched every corner for him. There was no sign of him. Then Alex noticed a small envelope lying on a table.

"They have mail service here too, huh?" John said as he came up.

Alex opened it. In a very beautiful handwriting it was written in 'Search for ME HERe→' and the arrow pointed to the door. In the envelope there was also a feather, probably used to write this message.

"It looks like a hawk's" said Alex studying it.

They walked towards the door. They glanced at the circular piece. They had to go through the door to reach Adrian. But which God to choose?

"Why don't we try all of them?" John asked Alex.

"Then why would he leave these clues?"

"Good point." John replied quickly.

"Why has he put the S, ME and HER in capital?" John asked himself.

Suddenly Alex went forward and just turned the circular piece. It stopped at 'Hermes'.

"This is the door." Said Alex.

"How do you know?"

"The Hawk's feather, the beautiful handwriting, the envelope, what do all these have in common?"

"Hermes? Oh, yes of course. He is the God of messengers and language and many other things and one of his sacred birds is a hawk. But what about the capital letters in the envelope?"

"It was written to search for him in here. In this circular wooden piece we rotate, right? Like that I just took the capital letters and put them here and there and got it." Alex clarified it to him.

"Shall we go inside?"

"Yeah, sure."

With their swords at one hand they opened the door. Inside a figure was standing at the far side of the room. One couldn't actually call it a room. It was very dark and one can't see the borders of the room. The only light was where the figure was standing.

With their blades raised they started moving in towards the figure. When they were a few meters away from the door, it closed with a creak. It all looked as if they were acting in a horror film and that they were in a very spooky house.

As they were walking Roark woke up. "Who turned the lights off? I can't see a thing." Roark groaned.

"Can you do something about it?" asked John.

Nemesis was also awake by then. "Let me see." Nemesis said.

Soon Roark and Nemesis started to glow faintly. But that was enough. They could see the floor. It was in dark tinted marble. They soon reached near the figure. The character was facing the other side. He was covered in spotlight. When they looked up there was no beginning for the light. It just happened to come from nowhere. They knew that it was not that important at that moment. The figure was wearing a dark robe. With his head down he turned towards them. They took a few steps back.

He spoke "I see that you are late." He had a dark, rough voice.

"We're sorry about that. But who are you?"

"Who I am is not important but who you are is important. I was sent by Adrian. I have to get you ready."

"Get ready for what?"

"Shut up and no talking." He was holding two bags. He whispered something. He then went near them and put the bags on them. Alex and John discovered that they couldn't move. The man had put a spell on them.

"You are now ready."

When he said this a long and wide tube appeared from above and covered both of them. As it fell they found that the spell had been lifted.

The man said "Don't pull it too soon."

"Don't pull what?" Alex asked.

He waved at them. Suddenly the place where Alex and John were standing disappeared. Before they knew it they were falling. It was a long way down. There were dark clouds around them. When they looked up there was nothing but the clouds. As they came down the clouds got lesser. A moment later Alex shouted to John in excitement "John, I see land."

John looked carefully and said "Don't get too excited. We're headed straight for the ocean."

"When should we pull our chute?"

"Remember the man said not to pull it too soon. Let's wait."

After some moments John shouted "I'm not an aviation expert but I think this should be high enough."

"Alright. On your mark. 3 2 1 **Go.**"

There was a chord hanging by their side. They pulled it. There was a sound from the bag. The next they knew was that they were flying. They were seated in a wooden chair. From the back of the chair two enormous wings sprouted. They started flapping and they went forward.

But when wings are flapped they instead of going up, they went sideways. Alex and John thought "This is not earth. This is some other place and anything can happen here"

John and Alex were moving to the land. On the arm rests of the seats, a small joystick appeared. John noticed that near the joystick, there was something written. When he observed it closer, in Greek it was written "A Hephaestus Product™"

On the other side Alex was learning to control the thing. They were over land by then.

"Let's take this thing down." John said. They descended towards the land.

As they neared the land they saw a magnificent palace. They landed just outside it. As they landed, the chair transformed into a bag again.

Except for the palace the place was full of mud. Between these mud heaps the palace was jutting out. A huge door and its walls stopped anyone from knowing what's going on inside. They went to find a way to get it open. It was hard to walk. At the door there was a small slot and on top of it was written 'Drop money here.'

John realized what it meant in a moment. "The drachmas!"

"But we didn't bring any of them." Alex said in dismay.

Suddenly the place started to rumble. They held onto each other. Dark energy was creeping up from one end of the wall. At the gate Alex and John were trying to find a way to keep steady.

Suddenly the rumbling stopped. They noticed that something was coming from the far end of the wall. Soon they could see a huge dark figure headed towards them. It was as huge as the wall itself. As it neared they pulled out their swords. They could then see the thing. They were frightened by it. It had legs and face of a mammoth, huge wing covered with fire, a huge tail with spikes at the end. It gave away a roar. Its stench was intolerable. Its saliva burned up the earth.

Alex and John were taken back by it. Alex turned the hilt of his sword. Once again Roark sprang to life.

When it took a glance at the creature, Roark too was surprised "Never thought they would be sending a Jorumnian now and it's humongous."

"Hey what are you blabbering about?" asked John expecting a strike any moment from the huge thing.

"Well, Jorumnians are basically children of the great sea serpent Jormungand. Remember when I told you that it was cut into many pieces and pieces became huge creatures. Well this is one of them. They are almost impossible to kill. See the armor that it wears? It would take you just your lifetime if you were to penetrate it. These things are very tough. There's just a problem with these things."

"And what would that be?

"They don't have anything in their brain. It sees anything, it attacks, whether it is doing any harm to it or not."

"So how do we defeat it?"

"There's no way we can defeat this thing."

Their conversation was broken up by a roar. They all turned to see what was happening. The thing did see them. It was charging towards them.

"What do we do?"

"I suggest that you fly away and keep your distance till something turns up."

"Alright."

John took a step back and was about to take off when Roark stopped them, "I think it will be good if you dodge when it is very near."

"Alright."

The Jorumnian leapt towards them.

"Take care, brother."

John warned his brother. Alex gave a nod. Just as the thing was about to smash them into pulp, they flew off in opposite directions. Instead of the taste of the human flesh which it was longing to taste, the Jorumnian got the dark mud up its tongue. It rose up in anger and frustration, searching for its prey's which were standing there just a moment before it crashed down into the earth.

It caught Alex flying alongside the wall. It straightened up its wings. The fire in its wings blazed up with pure energy coming from its heart. Just one swing and it was up and flying towards Alex. Alex was flying without knowing about the danger that was fast approaching. John, flying at a safe distance, was shouting to Alex to move away. Alex then felt a sudden heat at his back as if the sun itself was coming right at him. He turned to see from where this much heat was coming. At first he could not see because of the massive light that was passing through him. When his eyes adjusted, he saw the creature flying towards him.

Alex suddenly had an idea that would buy them some time. He stood just adjacent to the wall. The thing then came at him with full force. Just as it was about kill Alex, he moved out of the place and the huge creature got smashed up in the wall! Its horns dug deep into the wall and it was struggling to get its horns out. It pulled very hard but it seemed to remain pinned in there.

Alex flew to John.

"What should we do now?" Alex asked.

"Don't lose hope yet. That thing may be yet break free of its problems." John responded with a sly grin on his face.

Meanwhile the creature was struggling to get free. When it thought that all hope was lost, it spit on its horns. Alex and John, while thinking what to do, saw that the mammoth like creature was up again and was coming at them. When it neared they could see that its horns were broken and it was half the size they were before. As it was nearing, a faint light came from their back. They turned to see what it was. At the end there was a faint light coming from the surface. They caught the glimpse of the sun's first rays. The golden ball slowly rose up.

The huge Jorumnian had stopped to admire it that it didn't even notice the humans flying past it. When it had seen enough, it searched around for its prey's. When it turned around it saw the two little humans standing there at the wall again. It thought of nothing else and just flapped its wings and went straight for them. They again dodged from it and it hit the wall.

When it turned this time the sun's rays hit at something on the huge creature's neck and produced light enough for making them impossible to see.

"What is producing that much light?" Alex asked covering his eyes.

"I don't know. It may be its armor." John replied.

"It is not its armor. Jorumnian armors do not reflect light. They are made of some special material." Nemesis who was silent all this time spoke.

"I suggest that we take a closer look." John said.

"Yeah. We need to observe it closely. It can be a clue."

They went near it. The creature was too dazed to see because of the immense light the sun suddenly produced. Alex and John came to the side of the creature. When they looked closely, they saw some kind of circular pieces tied to a thread hanging from its neck. It was golden in color. They realized the moment they saw it. It was the Drachmas.

"Now I see why the sun rose. It wanted us to know that there are drachmas in the Jorumnian's neck. It wanted us to find it." Alex said.

The whole place was then bathed in the rays of the sun. The creature again focused on them.

"I'll distract it while you take the Drachmas." John said.

"Sounds like a good plan to me. You ready?"

"Ready when you are."

"Alright, let's go." John took off in one direction while Alex just stood there.

The creature caught one of the humans flying away. It was tempted. After all it had been rotting in a room two days before. A dark hooded figure had visited him and promised many treasures if it does exactly what the small figure demanded. The next day it was out in the world wearing full body armor searching for two humans. And what a coincidence is that it is just fighting two men fitting the description of what the small figure said. It knew that, after these silly humans die, it is heaven waiting for it. Right then all it needed to think was that one of the humans was escaping. It needed to go after him.

John was not going much far. He just kept circling around the creature at a distance. Alex was waiting for the signal from John. John meanwhile had got the creature following him. He went to the wall and just stood there. He had hoped for the creature to come after him and he would move from his place just in time so that the creature would hit the wall again and get stuck there just like Alex did.

But the creature suddenly stopped chasing John the moment he stood there at the wall. It cleared its throat and took a deep breath. John couldn't figure what it was going to do. As he watched a type of green slime came from the creature's mouth straight at him. It was too late. He had nowhere to move. He just closed his eyes.

Surprisingly he did not feel anything. When he opened his eyes the creature was there all right. When he looked down he saw a huge chunk of ice between him and the creature.

Alex was standing to one side of the monster. He quickly shot of a bolt of ice from his hand. It hit directly at the Drachmas. The thread broke unable to hold too much weight. It fell down. He flew down quickly and grabbed the Drachmas and went near John.

"Come on, are you going to stand there."

When they reached a safe distance Alex said to John "So much for your plan."

"Thanks for saving me. I guess we will have to wait now for the ice to melt."

"Not necessarily."

Alex then flew over to the creature. He climbed onto its back. He held out the sword over the flaming wings. All he had to watch out for was the tail of the creature which came to strike him now and then. Other than that he had to keep balance because the creature kept shaking itself.

The Jorumnian was still trying to make up what had happened. It never remembered about some gold coins at its neck. When the sun dawned on them its neck felt a little heavy. And right then one of the humans was on its back tickling him!

It tried to shake the man off, but it seemed as if the man was stuck to it. Alex quickly stabbed the tip of the sword into one of the eyes of the creature. It roared like anything with pain. It tried hitting with its tail but it didn't even touch the little man. It continued to shake and suddenly it felt relieved. It felt to it as if a huge burden was lifted. It watched with its other eye the man flying to join the other one.

"Ouch! What do you think of yourself, that you can do anything to us if we are some piece of steel? We also have feelings." Roark jumped at Alex.

"Sorry. After all it was for a good cause. We needed some time to escape from the creature. I am sure you will apologize to me." Alex said.

"Hmm. It's all right. I accept your apology but just for this once. If it wasn't for the ice, I would be gone now. You will be left with a well-built ordinary sword with nothing special about it. Alright now let's move on to the door." Roark said cooling down.

"Are you all right?" John asked Alex.

"Yeah I am perfectly all right."

They reached the door. The creature was still there. It had started to descend. Alex took one of the drachmas and inserted in to the given slot. For a moment there was nothing. Then they heard a deep sound 'Welcome'. Then the door opened with a long creak.

The huge door slowly opened. The creature was alerted by the sound coming from the door. When it looked closely it saw the humans getting inside quickly. It had to get inside if it had to kill them. It rose up and made a run for it. When it was halfway it saw that the door was closing. It sprinted even faster. Alex and John quickly closed the huge door. Just as they closed and turned to walk they heard a loud thud on the door. Nothing had happened to the door. It still stayed intact. That was one sturdy door and they walked forward.

CHAPTER THIRTEEN

"The Mission Begins"

THERE WAS A SMALL footpath of small gravels for them to walk on. There were small pots with colorful flowers all the way. Beside the flower pots and footpath the whole place was covered with fresh green grass. They walked on. A few meters ahead they saw a palace. It had a dome made of glass on the top. The whole thing was carved out of white marble. There were some brilliant carvings in the palace. There were many pillars in front of the main entrance.

They walked straight in. They were welcomed by a pointy eared dwarf wearing elfish like clothes. The dwarf was also incredibly white.

"Welcome. We were expecting you. Follow me." He said in a weird alien language.

They followed the guy without saying anything and guessing that it was a welcome call. They took many rights and lefts. Each time they reached a door, the dwarf murmured something and the door then quietly opened. At last they reached a long hallway. On reaching the end the dwarf again opened the door and said "From here you go yourselves." He pushed them inside and closed the door.

Where they were standing right then could not be called a room. It was a huge hall. There was the dome that they saw from outside. It allowed light to fall in which illuminated the hall. At the center there were two people arguing. John and Alex hid themselves behind a pillar and observed them. The two people were none other than Zeus and Adrian.

"They are going to come with you." Zeus made his stand firmly.

"But they have just arrived here. They are not that much strong. You know how dangerous this mission is." Adrian replied back.

"That is the exact reason why I am sending those two to this particular mission. You know about the oracle also"

"Oh, yeah? Just because their father is not going to . . ."

Zeus grabbed Adrian's mouth. "Didn't you hear what the elves said? They are going to be here any moment. This discussion is over. They are coming with you and that is that."

He slowly retreated his grab. They took their seats and waited.

"I think that's our cue." John said rising from his position.

"I think it will be better if we do not tell them that we heard the conversation." Alex said getting up.

They slowly came into the light. Zeus greeted them sitting "Welcome. I hope your journey was not uncomfortable."

"Nothing important. We just had a little problem at the entrance." Alex said.

"The elves treated you well, I hope." Zeus gave away a smile.

"Oh! They were marvelous." John said.

"Please. Have a seat. I am sure you will be starving. We can talk after that."

Zeus snapped his fingers. A table appeared. Elves broke in with plates laden with delicious and scrumptious food. They laid it on the table and went back quietly.

Alex whispered to John "Now that's a lot of silverware."

They sat and started to help themselves. The others just sat there waiting for them to finish. When they finally finished Zeus said "Oh, the wash basin is at the far end of the room."

Alex got up first. He went towards the wash basin. On the way there were many rooms. At one point Alex thought he saw a man wearing a black cap in a room. When he turned to have a good look at the room, there was not a soul to be seen in the chamber. By then John had caught up with Alex.

"What are you looking at?"

"Nothing. I thought I saw somebody in here."

"You're chasing ghosts, brother."

The wash basin was the only exceptional case in the building. It was fully modern. When they approached, it flickered to life. When they stretched out their hands, the water automatically started flowing. Alex thought "Motion sensing. A technology that will soon dominate 'our world'."

The water was crystal clear. When they got back, there was no table there, just two more chairs. They came and took their seats.

Zeus began "Alright, now that we are all here, let's talk business. I am sure that you have gained good training from Adrian and I shall proclaim that you are now fit to go for the mission. Are you ready for it?"

"Alright. We are ready to accept the task. But, what is it? What should we do?" John jumped in enthusiasm.

"I must warn you. This operation is utmost dangerous." Zeus said.

"We shall decide when we hear what it is." Alex responded.

"Alright. Here it is. I have good news and bad news for you. The bad news is that as I have already said, Poseidon was kidnapped by some of Cronus's forces. We want you to get him back."

"What's the good news?"

"The good news is that Adrian will be coming with you."

Adrian came forward. He noticed that there was not even a tinge of surprise for the brothers to hear it. It was as if they knew this was going to happen. Alex and John quickly tried to express some kind of surprise on their faces.

"How do we know were Poseidon is?" A question suddenly aroused in Alex's mind.

"There's no need to for you to search for him. He's being kept in Muspellheim."

"How did you come to that conclusion?"

"We have spies at our disposal. My father is an old fashioned guy. He still relies on the way the world was when I was born. But do not ever underestimate his army. They are all one tough nut to crack. We have captured them and have tried to leak any information we could in every possible way but they kept mum. So Adrian shall give the rest of the details and plan. You shall leave tomorrow at dawn." saying this Zeus immediately left the room. There was a total silence in the hall.

"So what should we do now?" John asked Adrian.

"Let's go and see some stuff."

He led them to a room. The room was painted white from floor to ceiling. Many kinds of weapons were kept there.

"We have heat seeking javelins, bazooka arrows, oh and this is a special one"

Adrian held up a tiny robot like thing.

"What does it do?" Alex asked.

"Well, this is a good spy. We can control it using this controller here. You see the eyes of it. Once active, they are like our own eyes. What it sees we too see! There's one more special feature. Now stand back."

Adrian cleared up some area and put the "robot" down. Then he pushed a little red button behind it and stood away from it. The little robot began to shake. The legs of it started growing. The metal in its hand turned and began to become bigger. There was a lot of gear work happening inside the little thing. Soon the little robot had become a big robot.

"Activate." Adrian said.

There were guns sticking out its hands. Lasers coming from its shoulders, there was a sword in its leg and a machine gun on its back. All in all it was a perfect killing machine.

"What's its name? Iron man?" John asked.

"You can call it whatever you like. This is our newest addition. For our mission we can take whatever we want from here. We shall set sail tomorrow." Adrian said.

"Set sail?" Alex asked doubtfully.

"Yes, we are going in a ship." Adrian said.

Their conversation suddenly broken by an elf "Sirs it is getting late. I came to remind you that night is going to fall soon. You may want to get some sleep."

"Yes we will only be a moment. Wait outside." Adrian said to the elf politely.

The elf bowed to them and went out.

"So that is all for now. Let's not waste our time admiring the weapons. We shall have lot of time for that on the way. Let's go."

He opened the door and led them out. The elf was obediently standing beside the door.

Adrian said to the elf "Show them their rooms."

"Yes, sir." The elf replied.

Adrian gestured for them to follow the elf. The elf started moving. They followed him silently. After many twists and turns they reached a room.

"This will be your room. Because of the short notice of your arrival we couldn't do much preparation. There is hot water in your bathroom should you bath. Your bed has been prepared. We hope you will find it cozy. You can put your armor and swords in the cupboard. There is tea brewing in the pot. Enjoy your stay."

The elf bowed to them and went back. Alex was the first into the room. It was big enough for two people. After they changed into their clothes, one by one they went to bath. They were very tired. They crashed into the bed as soon as they could.

CHAPTER FOURTEEN

"The Pirates And The Old Man"

T HEY WOKE UP EARLY the next day. When they looked out of the window they could see the emergence of the sun from the calm and silent sea. The sun's rays reflected upon the waves. It was a beautiful sight. As they were enjoying the moment, they were taken aback by a voice. They turned to see Adrian dressed up in full armor.

"It is a beautiful day to begin our journey." He greeted them.

"Yes, indeed it is a beautiful day. When are we going to be off on our journey?" Alex received him.

"As soon as you are ready. I have some things to attend to. You get ready and meet me at the entrance. Do not worry about your clothes and all. It's been packed and loaded into the ship."

After saying this Adrian left both of them to their business. After they had bathed, an elf came to their room to serve them breakfast. Soon they were at the entrance led by the elf. They had put on their armor as well. Adrian was waiting for them

"So, are you ready?" he asked them.

"Of course we are ready. Let's go." John said in excitement.

A carriage was waiting for them outside. It was pulled by two white and elegant horses. The elf who rode it climbed down and opened the doors for them to enter. It looked like they were in the early 19th century.

Adrian went in first. Then Alex and John went in. After they got seated in the soft cushion they felt the sedan move followed by a long creak which must have been the huge gate. They could not see what was outside as there were no windows in it. Then a sound came from the front which resembled of a sound of a bell.

Adrian said clutching on the handle bar above them "I would hold on to that if I was you."

They obeyed him. As soon as their hands touched the bars, the carriage leapt forward. They were taken aback. They got pressed in the cushion. It felt to them as if they were going in a warp. But it lasted only moments. Soon they were back in their original position. Suddenly they felt a thud at their feet.

"We have reached at the port. Let's go." Adrian stepped out.

John slowly peeped out.

"No need to be shy. Come on out." Adrian called out to them.

They slowly emerged out of the carriage. They strapped their swords to their belts. The port was a wonderful one. There were enormous ships as well small fishing boats. There were seagulls and many other birds flying around.

There were many distinctive creatures on the land yet they walked among everyone unnoticed. As a matter of fact most of the 'everyone' were creatures with shapes they could least imagine. There were many hawkers selling fishes or fish-like creatures. There were also many pubs where groups hung out and many inns. There were many building also which gave warriors on contract pay to people as escorts and all. Beyond the buildings was just barren land. There was a whole chaos in the place.

"Welcome to the port of Macmillan. This is where we begin our journey. Follow me."

They walked up to the end of the port. And there was a small row boat at the end. John spotted it from a distance itself.

Adrian said "There's our vessel."

John jumped at him "That thing? Seriously? You're kidding right?"

"No, I'm serious. I never kid." Adrian said.

"We are to go in that small piece of junk."

"Junk, what do you mean by it? This is the strongest there is."

"Oh, I can see how strong it is."

Alex broke their argument "Stop it, both of you. I believe you have a misunderstanding. John, would you be so kind to tell us which one you were referring to?"

John pointed to the small boat "That small thing."

"Oh, I get it. We were blabbering without even knowing what we were fighting for. I am terribly sorry. I was actually referring to this one over here."

Adrian pointed to a magnificent ship which was floating just adjacent to the small boat. It had huge rectangular masts. There were banks of some 30 cannons on both sides for broadsides firing.

"I welcome you aboard to the pride of our naval army, Zandra. She's a real beauty, isn't she?" Adrian said.

They were still awe-struck at the ship's sight.

"Yeah, she is."

"Come. Let's meet her closely."

They stood on a platform and pulled a rope which was tied up to the plank of wood. The platform slowly started to rise. Soon they were in the air and slowly rising up to the ship. When they reached parallel to the vessel, Adrian jumped and said "Come on, don't be shy, and jump."

John got excited and jumped. Though he landed safely, he put a force on the plank that made Alex hanging for life by it.

Adrian was shouting to Alex "Swing with all your might."

Alex did what he could. Soon he was moving like a pendulum. Adrian leaned over trying to catch hold of the plank but with no success.

"I can't reach it you have to use more energy" Adrian said.

"I'm doing all I can. I think I am going to be stuck here forever. Wait a minute. I am losing my grip. Somebody do something. I am going to fa . . ." and that was it.

Alex Blake went down. They both leaned over to see. But surprisingly all they could see was sea water receding back to the sea. Alex had gone under. John couldn't take it. He sat on the deck. Adrian tried to comfort him.

John pushed him aside "This is all because of me. I should never have jumped like that. This is entirely my fault. I would rather die instead of him."

John started crying. Suddenly a familiar voice came from behind "You would do that for me?"

John turned to see who it was. He saw a figure standing there in front of him. The sun's rays were gleaming from behind him. He wiped of his tears and stood up to watch who it was. It was none another than Alex. John ran and hugged him.

"What happened to you?" John asked him.

"My hand slipped and I fell after that what happened I am not sure." Alex said.

"But we saw you fall. How did you survive?"

"I don't quite remember. When I was falling it felt to me as if I was light as a feather. After that I found myself standing on the deck."

"Well what had happened had to be what it should have been. I suggest we better get in." Adrian said pointing to the dark clouds that appeared all out of a sudden.

Suddenly some men appeared from below. All of them looked tough. Alex and John were surprised by it. They quickly got to their feet. Adrian on the other hand, greeted them.

"Hey guys how are you? Do any ventures lately?"

A bald man came from among them and said "Hello Adrian. I welcome you aboard my dearest Zandra, once again."

"Hey, Nicholas, how are you?" Adrian replied.

The name Nicholas bore recognition to Alex and John. The conversation of Nicholas and Damen had helped them a lot. In fact if it wasn't for them they wouldn't even be here.

"Are these the men you told me about?" Nicholas asked him.

"Yeah these are the ones."

There was a crackling sound of thunder.

"I think it would be good if we go inside." Nicholas said.

He then shouted to his men "Men, let the sails free. Lift up the anchor. Let her feel the Ocean. We are going to have wind soon."

"Aye, Aye Cap'n." The men went to do their work.

"Come on let's go inside."

The captain led them into his cabin which was above the deck on a raised place. It was a small room. There was a table where he kept his instruments. The whole place was carved out of wood, perhaps cedar. There was a small shelf which held some books. They took their seats in front of the table. Nicholas cleared some of the items on the table and went to the end of the room. He returned with a pot and three glasses. He poured something steamy in it and served it to them.

"What is it" Alex asked him.

"Hot chocolate" Adrian said taking a sip of it.

Nicholas took an apple and took a bite of it. On the table there was a map of a world which looked familiar to both Alex and John but still they couldn't recognize it.

"If you don't mind, might I ask you where are we?" John asked politely.

"Why, we are in Earth. Didn't Adrian tell you that? We are at the western end of Africa." Nicholas informed them.

"Well I was going to tell you soon." Adrian said to both of them who had fixed their gaze at him.

"Where does this map show?" Alex asked the captain.

"It is earth. You must have got confused by the land that is there just adjacent to North America."

"Yeah, what place is that and why is there a skull on the place?"

"That place is where the Bermuda triangle is. That is the lair of our enemy. That is the only way through which one can enter Muspellheim. They have a powerful system there which will make even the Pentagon or the Kremlin look like idiots. Many brave men and woman, I might add, have gone there, but a handful of people have returned to tell the tale."

Adrian interrupted Nicholas "That is the place we are going. We came to ask your help to get us there. No one else in the whole world would help if they heard where we are going."

"No one else would be crazy enough to go there. You think I would simply put me and my men in the hands of death?" the captain's voice changed from sweet to a sudden stern voice. But Nicholas didn't tell why he agreed for the trip. Alex and John were wondering why he agreed if that is for sure that he will not return.

He then went out and called one of his men "Henry come here."

A man who was tending to the sails came up to him.

"You called me, sir?" he humbly said.

All three of them inside could hear what they were saying.

"Yes, I want you to show these men the guest's room. They will be coming with us to the Bermuda triangle."

Henry went in and came out with Alex and John. They went through a couple of stairs below the deck and after that through a small hall way. On the way they saw small cabins, compact but they looked cozy. Their rooms were much bigger than that. It was big enough for them.

Henry left Alex and John to do his own work. They removed their armor and kept it on a table provided. When Alex opened the glass windows in the room, a gust of wind dropped in. He could also hear the shouts of the men above them "pull up the anchor, we are sailing." "Hard to starboard."

There was heavy rainfall on the place. Waves hit the ship rocking it. Long and strong oars appeared from their sides. Strong hands pushed them hard into the sea. They were favored by the winds. Soon they were out in the sea. Alex closed the window just before a sea gull came to perch on it.

A man came and called them for lunch. When they were back in the deck the rain had cleared and the sun had come out. They could see the port far away. They were to have lunch at the captain's cabin. The captain welcomed them. They sat on a round table. A man came in and served them their lunch. It was not much heavy but enough. After the lunch, they went out on to the deck. The men were at ease as they had no work to do. They sat in groups and chatted. Adrian went back to his room. Seeing Alex and John coming out the sailors called out to them "Hey, do you want to come over?"

"Yeah, sure, why not?" John, as always jumped.

Before Alex could call him back, he had already reached near the sailors. When Alex had reached there he found John sitting on top of a barrel and already in a chat.

"Come on. Have a seat." One of the sailors offered Alex a barrel.

John asked the sailors "How well do you guys know Adrian?"

"Well, we first met him as an apprentice of the legend, Mr. Blake. Lucky guy, this Adrian, to be an apprentice of someone of that much importance."

"What happened to him?" Alex asked.

"Adrian?"

"No, Sir Blake"

"Well, we all remember what happened to him. It was on that bloody night that we all saw last. We were sailing like usual on that day as per a plan of Mr. Blake and Adrian. At night when we were all asleep, a loud thud came from the deck. All of us woke up and went to the deck. It was raining hard. When we reached there we found a body lying on the deck. The captain had also come by then. We closed in towards the body. Suddenly there was a slight movement in it. Soon he stood up. We went and took a coat and a mug of hot, sizzling coffee was served. He drank up the coffee greedily and threw away the mug. Somebody brought a lantern. That was when we realized that it was none other than Sir Blake. We were surprised, taken aback by it."

He stopped for a while and continued.

"It was said that Sir Blake had found a way to put an end to Cronus and his rule once and for all. Our sail was part of it. Though we heard about him, we had never seen him and wanted to see him at least once. It was at that time that he tumbled upon our ship. But when we saw, he was looking upset and said he had betrayed his family and that he is never going to forgive himself for doing that. Till then no one ever knew that he had a family. He said his sons will once deliver his plan as he has become weak or made weak by someone. After that he started to glow. There was fire all over him. We all took a step back. Then in a flick of an eye he was gone. That was the last that anyone saw him"

"And what happened to Adrian?" John asked.

"He became our captain. Recently it was said that Mr. Blake's two sons were found. Now we have to get them first or else Cronus's forces will take them."

"Why would they be interested in those two people?" Alex was thriving to know the truth that was hidden from them.

"As we said earlier Blake told that the sons will complete his plan, which was confirmed by an oracle too. Have you guys by any chance seen the Blake brothers?"

Then suddenly the captain interrupted them "They are the sons of Blake."

"Oh my god, really? It is an honor."

They all stood up and greeted the captain.

"At ease, men." he sat down.

The others followed.

"I couldn't get to know you guys properly yesterday, so I might as well make the best out of this opportunity." The captain said.

Alex and John just heard a faint sound of the metal hilt of Nicholas before they fell down. The first they saw was Nicholas's swords at their neck. Just then Adrian came and stopped Nicholas. He then helped them up and said to the captain "They are just kids. They will never be your match".

"Well. I was just going easy on them. I just had to see if they had the power and strength of their father."

He turned to them "If you continue to be like this, then you will be disgracing your father's name and pride. God knows where the poor man is now. You shall need more training friends and I will be kind enough to provide it to you. So tomorrow the first thing you do in the morning is meet me here, lads. Now; I have to go".

Adrian came close to them "Listen carefully. He is not going to go easy on you. So, train carefully. If you do you may have a slight chance of touching me with your sword."

He then went to the edge and just enjoyed the sea. The others went to their usual jobs. The day went over quickly. It was a pleasant day next morning. When Alex and John got ready, Adrian came inside their room, fully armored. His armor was shining like anything and he was panting.

Adrian said "Get dressed up quickly. We have located pirates up ahead. I don't think they will let us pass without a fight. We are gathering up all we can. Come to the deck quickly."

Saying this he went out of the room. Alex and John had just got up. They got surprised by it. However they got the message. They acted quickly. Soon they were fully dressed up. With their helmets in one hand and their swords on the other, they went up.

The scene looked as they were preparing for a war, which was actually they were here for. The captain was standing in the middle of the deck with Adrian giving orders to his men. His men were running here and there with all kinds of weapons. Someone was loading the cannons while some others were getting the swords and lances from cargo hold. There was a whole chaos in the place but still everybody worked with perfect unison. Alex and John went up to Nicholas and Adrian.

"Well, lads I guess there isn't enough time for me to train you properly, so you just watch me and act. I can guarantee you one thing my friends, today you will know why my ship is the number one in the navy."

Then he shouted to his people "Men, these two lads here doesn't know the power of Zandra. Let's be kind enough to show them. What do you have to say about that, huh?"

There was a huge roar from the men.

"Not only will these two, the pirates also know the might of us. Because they are going to be crushed into pieces and not us, their ship will sink and not ours. Alright, so what are you waiting for, put a step on it. We got some fighting to do."

Nicholas's encouraging speech put energy into the men that sent them flying into their positions.

Then Nicholas said to Adrian and the two others "Adrian, I want you to take the middle side with some of my men, while I will take the back side and you two will be handling the rest. Don't worry, that's were the least men be."

"How much is this 'rest'?"

"Nothing big, just front side, the deck and the cannons, nothing serious to worry about" he said it as it was just a walk in a park.

The pirate ship was clearly visible then. As it approached cannons from the Zandra emerged. They were forged from tough metal. Anyone who saw it could understand that they meant business. There were also three small cannons which revolved as they shot. They were all that were needed to bring a ship down. On the deck, the men were ready in their positions, so were the pirates.

On their ship, a man was shouting to his men "Remember men, we are here on a job and we will finish it. Do not forget what awaits us if we are able to pull this off. There will be no more pirating and getting chased by the navy. We will be free from all this mess once and for all. One more thing. This thing you're in is voluntary. No one forcefully put you in this. So anyone who wants to turn back can do so now. Is there anyone?"

The men stayed still.

"Thought so. Now move your bodies. Remember we will take only what we want and nothing else. Let's go now. We got fighting to do." He finished.

By then Zandra had reached adjacent to the pirate's ship. Cannons from both the ships burst to life. After the first volley, the pirates who were hiding behind their sails came out with ropes on everybody's hands which were tied to the mast. With it they jumped into their enemy's ship. The men in the Zandra were expecting this. They fell back to the center of the deck immediately. They took out their spears and held it high. It was unexpected for the pirates.

But they knew better. When they reached the edge of the deck they cut their ropes so they landed safely on the ship safe from the spears or the sea. But not for long. The others then used a better formation to attack the pirates. Then the captain and the others slowly advanced in this formation.

But the pirates were prepared for that too. From their ship volleys of arrows appeared which was actually unlikely of pirates. They were usually reckless people who attacked with no mind. But here it was a new array of these kinds of people. Though the arrows managed to put down some of the men but most of the others wore heavy armor.

The men on Zandra replied with crossbows which were loaded and kept there. The archers on the pirate ship went by the huge bolts the crossbows shot. The captain tried to fend them off with the spears, but they didn't seem to budge. So he ordered all his men to put down their spears and bring out their swords. Then the real fighting started. Both parties broke off their groups to fight.

In a few seconds there was blood everywhere. To Alex and John it was quite an experience. There was shouting and clashing of metals and the sound of the cannons in the background. It rocked the ship. More and more pirates started coming in from the ship. The two brothers could see Adrian fighting and killing with swift strokes which never missed its target. On the other hand Nicholas was not bad either. His strokes cut through the enemy with ease. The others were also aggressive fighters. Only Alex and John were the shy ones who stood at the center of the deck with their swords.

"Come on. We have to get in that fight, not sulking here." Roark was nagging at Alex.

Suddenly Nicholas came to them "We can't hold them off forever like this. We have to bring their ship down and you are the guys best suited for the job."

"What do we have to do?"

"You will have to go to secret cargo hold."

"Where is it?"

"As a matter of fact, it happens to be straight under the pirates."

"And you want us to go there. What's in it anyway?"

"If I told you, would it be a secret anymore? Anyway, you go down there. You will see a lever at the far end of the room. You pull it and come back here. We will give you 5 minutes' window. That's all we can give you. Come and fight these pirates. When the window comes, you do what I told you. All of us are counting on you. So, you ready?"

"I guess."

"I'll take that as a yes. **ATTACK!!**" he ran straight into the fight.

They followed. Some pirates saw them and quickly charged at them. Alex and John got frightened. But they didn't display it on their faces and started fighting bravely. The pirates were taken aback by their fighting. They knew that these two could fight. But here they were putting down their men one by one. Thanks to Roark's guidance they both did brilliantly. More and more pirates started coming from the ship. The others wondered how one ship could hold this much men. But they could easily hold them. The sight of their captain, Adrian and the other two in the front lines encouraged them to fight. But how much could they take?

Soon they had taken almost all of the deck back. Alex and John could go down the secret cargo hold. Going down the ladder they got the smell of grapes down in the room. Roark and Nemesis started glowing. It was enough to light up the whole room.

They saw many crates on the place. They went near one. There was something written on it. It was marked '**GERMANY**' on it. They could easily guess what was in it. The smell of the grapes. Crates from Germany. They were surprised how captain of a ship of the navy could say that his secret cargo hold is full of these. But then, they are, after all, sailors. What more could you expect from them?

John and Alex walked up to the end of the room. A small lantern lighted the place. Under it, in a small glass case was a lever. Alex opened it.

Suddenly Nicholas's voice came from the deck "Pull it guys. We can't hold them off anymore."

Wasting no time, Alex pulled it. They were curious about what was going to happen, so they ran out to see it themselves. When they reached the deck, it was clear of pirates, but more were about to come when they stopped and stared at something on the Zandra. Alex and John leaned to see what was happening. As they looked a metal rod emerged from the ship. It extended and hit the pirate ship's hull. It pierced the hull.

Nicholas had a controller with which he controlled the movement of the rod. The tip of the rod was then turned down and it went straight for ship's bottom. After it went through it, Nicholas pushed a button on the controller and the tip expanded to become a five pointed star. Nicholas then pushed another button and the rod started retreating. It made huge hole in the pirate's ship as it came back and soon water started filling it. The rod went back into Zandra.

Everyone involved in the fight watched as the pirate's ship sunk. The captain of the pirates stood simply at the deck doing nothing. His men too, surprisingly did nothing. Some of the men just prayed.

Alex went straight to Nicholas "This was your idea?"

"Yeah."

"Isn't this cheating?"

"I call it improvising"

John then came and asked Nicholas "Why did the pirates do nothing as their ship sunk?"

"They never surrender; neither a surrendered pirate is pardoned. The sure death made them face it calmly"

It took less than fifteen minutes for the pirate's ship to sink with the pirates. Alex and John felt a bit upset seeing the pirates sinking with the ship without a fight.

Then suddenly one of Nicholas's men came up to them and said "Sir, most of our food resource is just gone. We are trying to figure out what happened. Nobody knows what happened to it."

"Alright. We will see to it. How much long till the rations end?"

"Two to three days maximum, sir."

"Alright. We will sail in search for land now. You may leave now."

He then turned to Alex and John "Well, you heard about the situation. So, the destination has changed. We are going to find some piece of land where we can find some resources. Once we do, we shall take you to Muspellheim. So how was our fight today? Are you now convinced that we are not just some blockheads from the navy and that we can fight?"

"Um . . . Yeah."

"Yeah? Come on lads. What happened earlier was more than just 'yeah'. Alright. Now. Are you guys tired?"

"Somewhat."

"Then you come to my cabin. I will serve you hot chocolate. You should also come, Adrian. You look tired in that armor of yours."

"Thanks. But I will help myself. I am going to have a look at our rations."

"Alright. If you need anything, I will be at my cabin."

Adrian went down to his room to remove his armor. The others went to the captain's cabin. It had the smell of hot chocolate when they entered the place.

"Can I ask you something, Nicholas?" John asked while Nicholas was taking out the pot.

"Yeah. Sure."

"Do you love chocolate very much?"

"What made you think so?"

"Well, your cabin smells full of chocolate and there is always chocolate brewing in that pot of yours."

"Well, you are right about it, lad. I love chocolate more than anything. I suppose you might be meeting the first captain who likes chocolate. You may even think I am crazy."

"No. it's all right."

The captain then served two cups with hot chocolate up to its brim. He also gave them some buns.

"You know, you guys are good people. I'll let you in on one of my secrets."

"One? How many do you even have?" John asked

"Do you want to hear it or not?"

"Sorry. Go on."

"Do you know what is in those crates in my secret cargo hold?"

"Yeah, we do."

"You do? Did you open it and looked in it?"

"No, we knew what its contents are the moment we saw where the crates came from and the smell which came from the room."

"Well then, let's hear it. What is inside it?"

"It is wine, isn't?"

"Whoever put an idea like that in you?"

"Well, there is the smell of grapes and the crates come from Germany. We know that Germany is famous for its wine."

"The explanation's quite good, but you are wrong. I shall prove it to you. Come with me."

Saying this he went out of the cabin. They followed him. They went down the stairs on the deck into the secret cargo hold. Nicholas put on the lights. He then took a crowbar lying there and went straight to the nearest crate.

The other two followed him silently all the way. Nicholas hit the crate's edges with the crowbar and the lid came off.

"You look for yourself what's in it."

They peeped into it. They saw huge packets in it. The label on the packet said 'Chocolate'.

"You bought chocolate from Germany?"

"Yeah."

"But why Germany?"

"Because you get the best chocolate of the Swiss from Germany. They are neighboring countries."

"Well, then. I guess we owe you an apology."

"Keep it for now. You may need it later."

They then went back. The men were working. There was a man on the nest up the mast looking for land or any ship. There was not much for Alex or John to do.

In the evening they went to the deck again. They watched at the beautiful sunset as the orb of fire died and slowly went down only to come back the next day.

John broke the beautiful moment "Should have brought a camera."

Then Adrian came from behind them and frightened them.

"Do you mind to share with me some of your moment?"

"Why not? Come on." Alex welcomed him.

"Can I ask you something?" John asked.

"Sure. Anything."

"At the place where Zeus gave us our mission, we had slightly eavesdropped in to your argument. Why did you not let us come on this mission?"

"Well, first of all, it is very dangerous. You may get yourself killed. Then there's one more thing. I too was at Nicholas's ship when your father, you know, disappeared. We all want Cronus's forces to die. So, I didn't want anything to happen to you guys."

Though not convinced with the answer, John asked "Why you and my father did go to the island where my father . . . disappeared? But is it not a fact that he died on that day?"

"Oh . . . That you will understand later. But I will tell you something. It is regarding the diamond that you discovered. Your father was after it. He said he needed it for building some plan to destroy Cronus. Anyway we will discuss these later." Adrian stopped abruptly.

The sun had set by then and darkness had crept in. they went inside to have their dinner. At the dinner, the captain had a whole chocolate cake with chocolate toppings, and every part of the cake was made from chocolate. After it, Nicholas went straight to his cabin to have a cup of chocolate.

When John asked one of his men about their captain's habit he said "You know, we have an extra cook just to make him his delicacies. Lord himself only knows where all the chocolate he eats goes."

After this all of them went to sleep. The next morning Alex and John woke up hearing a shout "Land. We have found land." In another five minutes they were up in the deck. They were hoping to see a small island a little away. But to their surprise, they found it actually quite near. In the night when all were sleeping, the ship came and crashed gently on the island. The men had already set up some ladders for the men to go down.

Just then Adrian came from the captain's cabin. He was carrying a map with him. When he saw them, he went straight for them and said "Hey, just woke up?"

"Yeah. What's that in your hands?"

"It's a map. I was just consulting it to see which island this is? Surprisingly, we shouldn't have found an island like this on our path."

"So, this thing just happened to come out of nowhere?"

"Sort of. Don't you want see the island?"

"Of course."

"Then move your body and get ready. Are you going to come in those robes?"

They quickly went to their room and got ready. In a few minutes they were back in the deck. This time Nicholas was also there. He had packed for himself some packets of chocolate in his bag. All of his men had put on their armor. One by one all of them went down the ladder. Two of Nicholas's men remained behind to watch over the ship.

Nicholas and Adrian were the men to lead the party. Alex and John were just behind them. The rest followed these men. The beach of the island had beautiful golden sand. A little in and the place was dense forest. The party went straight for the wilderness. There were all kinds of wild plants and trees around them. The leaders were creating a path with their swords not only for the others to follow, but also to find their way back. They walked on for some minutes.

Meanwhile back in the ship, the two men who remained back there couldn't close their mouths. They were watching as one of the mountains on the inland of the island started to show the indication to explode. Just when one of them was about to get down to warn the others, the mountain exploded!

Lava burst out of the peak. Huge chunks of rocks started flying out of the top. The man returned back to the ship. They could only pray for their safety. Meanwhile in the dense forest, the ground started to break. They were too concerned about their safety that they didn't know what was going to happen. Suddenly the earth split and divided the party. Alex and John were on one side while the others managed to get on the other side. No one could get to the other side as the gap made was filled with hot, boiling lava. It was miracle that nobody was hurt in this mess.

Though they were separated, they could speak to each other.

"Are you guys all right?" Adrian asked them

"Yeah, we are all right. How about there?"

"Nothing serious here. Every body's fine. Listen, we are on the side where we created the path. We can get back easily. But what about you? What will you do?"

"We shall walk alongside the lava and reach the shore. Then we shall come to you. So, I think you should be heading back to the ship. We will be along soon. We will be alright." Alex said.

"Are you sure you will be fine?"

"Yeah. How hard can it get?"

"You don't know, lad. This is the real world and unknown too. Lord knows what will happen to you. But here we do not have any other choice."

"So we shall meet again at the ship. You wait for us there, okay?"

"Okay. So that's fixed. Bye now."

They then went to their separate ways. Alex and John just followed the flowing lava. They went on when they reached a clearing. There was a small house there. There was smoke from the top.

"Who could possibly be living here? Should we go in?"

Suddenly Nemesis spoke "I think that's dangerous. We should avoid it."

"I think it will be alright" Roark said.

"I think you're right, Roark. What harm has ever come in visiting a house?" John said this and took the next step on the cleared are.

Suddenly a lasso which was hidden in the grass came up and in a matter of seconds John was hanging on top of a tree. As Alex watched, John got dragged and went into the house. Alex could only watch.

Alex then carefully moved towards the house. Surprisingly nothing happened to him. He reached safely at the door. He knocked at the door. Suddenly, the planks under which he was standing disappeared. Alex only had the time to tell "Oops." He went rolling down a long tube. Soon the tube widened and Alex fell on a soft cushion like thing. It was too cushiony that he couldn't even stand upon it. Then a rope came from the top and tied him up. It then lifted him up. The surroundings then changed. He was then sitting tied up in a chair inside a room. John saw him. He too was tied up.

In a table in front of them, were two cups full of tea. On the other end sat a man. He had a beard. He looked much older than them. Even though they were seeing this guy for the first time, he seemed familiar. They both tried to recall who he was but they couldn't.

"Don't try and mess up your brain trying to remember who I am. You will reach nowhere with that. Now, do you mind telling me the purpose of your visit to my island and please, have some tea. It will become cold before you know it. Please apologize for my traps. Cronus is after me for the past few months. He keeps sending his monsters." The man said to them.

Alex noticed the heads of monsters hung on the wall "Did you kill all these monsters?"

"Yeah with my swords right here."

He pointed to pedestal near the wall. On it were 2 swords kept crossed. He went and took it and walked to them.

"Do you want to see how I sliced down 2 monsters head down in just one slash?" he then went behind them and then swiftly cut both of the ropes that had bound them.

They were free. Alex asked him "Why did you cut these ropes?"

"I felt that you both have heart. But I also felt something else."

"What was it, tell us."

"Oh, I guess your tea has gone cold. Let me go and heat it up for you."

He took the cup and went to the back side of the house. From there he called out to them "Why don't you take a look around my house while I am busy here"

Alex and John rose from their place. Nemesis then whispered to them "Now that he has gone into the kitchen, I suggest that this is the best opportunity for us to escape. I sense an evil presence in him."

"Oh, really. I think he is just a nice guy." Alex replied back.

"And I think it is the first time you have ever sensed an evil presence in anyone." John said

"You are wrong and earlier there was no reason to warn you. But this, this is the real world and you need to look out." Nemesis said.

"No, you are wrong and besides, we want to know more from him. He knows something of us that we don't know. So just keep your voice low till we get out".

Roark lay silent all the time. After John said this they went to look around his house. They first went to the wall on which the man kept the heads of monsters as souvenirs. Then they went to the pedestal where he kept his swords. The blades had elaborate carvings. As they were strolling through his house, watching all the types of souvenirs and the pictures of him killing the monsters, he came with cups of tea. There was steam coming from it. He quickly kept them on the table.

Alex asked him "Why do you have all these pictures when you have the real thing on the wall."

"Well, that's proof that these heads are not fake. What would I say to someone who would come in my house and say that these are just sham. You tell me, huh? What would I say?"

"Alright, you made your point."

"Now, where was I?"

"You said you felt something . . ."

"Oh, yes. I remember now. You have good heart. But there is something bad too. You both will be betrayed by the one you call a friend."

"Can you tell us who it is?"

"I am sorry. I don't have that power. Excuse me, what did you say you name were?"

"My name is John and this is my twin brother Alex."

"John and Alex? Oh yes, John and Alex. You are the sons of Blake, right?"

"Yeah, the same."

"Wow, I never thought I would see you guys again."

"Again? You know us?"

"Well, I knew your father very well."

"How well?"

"I knew him better than anyone else. But I can tell you that his death was a fake. I too have a role in that."

"Did our father tell you to do that?"

"Yeah." He was showing interest to stop the conversation.

"Do you know where he is now?"

"I am sorry but I can't help you with that. What I can say, he visits me sometimes. I saw him just last month."

"So you don't know where he lives?"

"No. But when he does come, he always talks about you two."

"How does he know about us?"

"Well, what do you think? A father will just give away his two sons to the world while he escapes? The reason why no monsters have been attacking you is because your dad is protecting you both from them. Even now you are under his protection and your enemies know it. He has kept an eye on both of you from the day he left you. He had always kept his distance. When he comes here to take rest for a day or two, he tells me all your stories."

"Who are you?"

"I've been a mystery to your father itself, so I don't see a reason to disclose my identity. By the way do you know Cronus is after you?"

"Could you help us by telling why?"

"That only your father knows. He only told me that he is building a big plan that will stop Cronus and his forces. He also said that, now only his descendants can complete the plan, as he had been cheated by a friend. By the way, how did you reach here?"

"We were on our way to Muspellheim when we found your island."

"Why?"

"Poseidon was kidnapped. Zeus ordered us to go find him."

"Zeus? That old guy? Anyway are you going alone?"

"No, we are going with Adrian in a ship captained by Nicholas."

"Adrian I remember. Good friend of your father. This Nicholas sounds familiar but can't quite recall him."

"He loves chocolate very much."

"Oh yes, I remember now. It was on his ship that everyone last saw your father."

"Was that you there too?"

"Of course not. That was your father himself".

John took a glance out through the window. They were busy talking that they didn't know about their surroundings.

"Alex, look outside, we are late. They will be worrying."

"Yeah, you're right. So, old man, I guess this is farewell to you."

"But you haven't drunk the tea yet."

He took a glance at it. "Though it is cold, you please have it" He insisted. John looked at Alex.

"Oh, never mind. I won't forget to mention about your visit. But then, he is probably up in one of those trees watching you. Now, at least have a sip of my tea" he insisted.

Alex and John sipped the cold tea and they felt a strange feeling of energy pouring in.

He walked them to the door.

"Hey, is there any trap in front of the house because I don't want to be going back in through the tube to the large hall." Alex said doubtfully.

"No my son, you don't need to worry about that. I wish you all the best on your journey".

Just when they took a step outside the old man said "Hey, one more thing. You must have heard the phrase

'Keep your friends close and your enemies closer'"

"Yeah."

"Well, you're doing exactly that. So keep knowledge of the company you keep. I am sure you will find out the truth very soon enough."

He closed the door. They were left on themselves again. They again followed the trail.

"I think we should keep this meeting of ours with the old man a secret."

"I too was thinking about that, considering what he said to us."

They reached the shore soon enough. They then saw the sunset. It was more beautiful than it was on the ship. They could see the ship lying there on the shore. As they approached, Adrian came down to get them.

"What took you so long?"

"A weed caught in John's leg."

"Come up. Everyone is anxious."

There was a sigh among the sailors when they saw Alex and John's face emerging from the ships rails. The captain came up to them.

"You had got scared for a little time, lads."

Then everything was back to normal again. Men started working on the ship. They had found food when they were coming back. Besides they could always catch fish. They also found the perfect wood for repairing their ship. Zandra had been damaged by the pirate's attack. They planned to set sail the next day. After dinner, Nicholas went to his cabin to his usual work. The rest went to sleep.

CHAPTER FIFTEEN

"The Whirlpool"

THE NEXT DAY MORNING was a pleasant one. Everyone woke up early despite the last day's tiredness. The men were busy trying to get the ship back into the ocean. With the help of the sea and the wind they easily, got the ship away from the island. They were back in the sea. Alex and John did some more fighting with Nicholas. Most of the time they were on the deck. After their training they sat beside the rails to take rest.

"You want to know a fact, lads?" Nicholas said.

"Why not" Replied Alex.

"There are two women that all the sailors in the world depend upon."

"All of them?"

"Yeah, all of them."

"Who are you talking about?"

"One is the sea and the other is their ship."

"You're absolutely right."

"Just imagine where man would have been if he had not learned to travel through the vast and beautiful sea."

"We wouldn't have to depend upon them?"

"Come on man, I told you to imagine. You're ruining the moment, man. Just close your eyes and feel it".

They did as he said. But they could not feel the sea as Nicholas said, but the men chattering, the sound of the wind and moreover their own thoughts. But not for Nicholas. He was silently concentrating on the sea and the sea alone. He removed all the thoughts from his mind and listened to the enormous ocean. He was fully devoted to it. He was what every sailor should look up to.

The others then realized that he was not just a block head who loved to have chocolate all the time. Even though they called Nicholas, he didn't hear them. Seeing him, they decided not to disturb him anymore and tried themselves to be like him. When they concentrated, slowly all the other sounds started to fade away. The chattering, the wind, and all other sounds and thoughts started fading. At the end, all they could hear was the sound of the waves hitting each other, the ship itself and the ship cutting through the water. They could only hear these. They both heard nothing else that they didn't even hear Nicholas calling him. When he shaked them, they jumped.

"You learned it, yes? Well, that's good for you. It will help you greatly in future. You can focus on what you want. I learned to do it by days of practice, but you lads have accomplished within an hour. How did you guys do it?"

"We don't really know. We just followed what you said and it all slowly came to us."

One of Nicholas's men barged in to their conversation

"Sir, you may want see this."

"What is it?"

"It's a little problem".

All of them followed the man. He went to the raised deck where the wheel was. From here, one could see all what was laying ahead. All the dangers that the sea had laid out for them!

Alex and John followed the captain and his men there. They hoped to see some very big problem which lay ahead of them, but surprisingly all they could see was the vast and calm sea.

But the look on Nicholas's face told them that something was not right. They could see his face in a panic feel. One of his men gave him a small telescope. When he looked through it, his panic only increased. He sent one man to fetch Adrian immediately.

Meanwhile Alex and John came up to Nicholas, and asked what the matter was.

"What is it, Nicholas? You look frightened."

"Have a look."

He gave John the telescope. Alex couldn't wonder the reason why both Nicholas and John were panicking. When his turn came, he found the reason. He too started to panic. Not so far away from the ship, a whirlpool was brewing on the path they had to go. If they were to go in to that God knows what will be left of them.

Adrian came then. When he heard the situation, surprisingly, Alex and John noticed not much surprise in his face. It was as if he knew it was going to happen.

"What can we do about this situation, Nicholas? Can we turn back?" Adrian asked.

"I'm afraid nothing much can be done. We can't turn back. There's too much wind. Even if we put our masts down, there's no chance to get away from this. We are going at a great speed. There's no way we can stop it now."

"How about going adjacent by it and just avoiding it?" John suggested.

"Good idea. But by the looks of it, by the time when we reach there, it would become very big and it will engulf us."

"How about we freeze the water?"

"So what you're saying is that you are going to freeze the whole sea with your magic. Sorry, not possible. Even if it was, I wouldn't allow you to do so."

"So, what should we do? Sit tight and hope for a miracle?"

"No lads, we are not cowards like you."

"Hey, who told you we are cowards."

"Do you want to hear this or not?"

"Of course. Continue."

"So, now that the whirlpool has proposed a new threat to us, we are not going to turn back or go by its side or sit tight. We are going to go in it."

"Wait. I think is it my ear's problem. But did I just hear you say that we are going through the whirlpool?"

"Your ear may have problem, lad. But you heard it correct and not through. We are going in it. There's a difference."

"But that is insane."

"I know. That's exactly why I am doing it."

"But . . ."

"Then you suggest an idea, lad."

"When did this crazy stunt even became an idea?"

Adrian interrupted them. He was thinking while the others argued.

"You know, it might work."

"Finally. Someone there who understands. Alright Adrian, explain to them why it will work."

"Why me? You are the one who thought of it."

"But you are the one who said it's a good idea."

"So?"

"So that means that you know about the idea and now you are going to spit it out."

Alex and John felt something fishy in their conversation. It was like a predetermined conversation.

All of a sudden the ship started to rock. One of Nicholas's men came to report "Sir, the current has caught us. It's too strong, sir. We have lost control of the ship"

While they had been arguing, the whirlpool had become a lot bigger. It was swirling with all the energy it has, ready to devour anything which comes in its path. As the ship closed in more, it was like a giant looking down upon a small man. All the men on the ship knew that their death was certain. Yet, their loyalty to their captain told them to move on. The vortex was almost near them. They had started to spin a little. Aboard the ship, everyone was busy trying to save their lives.

The captain was yelling to everyone "hold on tight to anything you can find. One more thing lads. Suppose we don't . . . you know, survive. I want all of you to know that we had a great run together. You were the best men that any captain could have. Now, brace yourselves".

Zandra rocked pretty badly. Many things flew out of the ship. Everyone either held on to the rails or the mast. The vortex slowly engulfed them. Everybody held their breath and hoped for a miracle. Alex was wondering if the so called 'idea' will work or not. But after a few moments in the sea water and he fainted.

The whirlpool then disappeared. It was as if it had come only to destroy Zandra. When Alex later opened his eyes, he was on a shore. The sand was sticking on to his face. It was dark too. He slowly rose up. He saw many planks lying on the shore. He slowly rose up. Nicholas's men were lying there, scattered here and there. A little bit away, others were also lying. A bit more and there was John. He had also stood up and was closing in on him. They woke up all the others.

The first thing the captain said was "Where's my dear Zandra."

"I guess she couldn't withstand the pressure. After all we came down through a whirlpool." Alex said.

"And survived too" Adrian very calmly added.

"Why is everything in this place so dark? Even the water is black." John asked.

"That's because we are in Muspellheim!"

"But how?"

"I will tell you one thing. When all this mess is over and if you survive, I will tell it to you then."

"Hey, sorry to interrupt, but didn't you say that Muspellheim was not just the underworld anymore."

"Did I say that? OK, maybe these are the parts still not cleared."

"Alright. Now that we are here, what do we do?"

"I say we gather whatever is left from the wreck and may be we can find something edible in the place. Then we camp here for the night and scour the place in the morning. But you remember, we have a mission here in Muspellheim?"

"So you knew it well that Zandra will enter the whirlpool?"

Adrian just smiled and said "Sounds good to me. Well, what are you waiting for? Let's go."

Everyone was busy again. They picked up everything along the shoreline and brought it to a little cave that they had found a little in. Night fell upon them soon. But there was not much difference. Everything was dark all the time. But when the breeze flew among them, it sent shivers down their spine. Inside the cave, they had managed to make a fire. Everyone was sitting around it warming them. They cooked some fish that they had caught in the evening which was black too. But it tasted good. Everyone had their fill and went to sleep. Each of Nicholas's men kept guard while the others slept.

CHAPTER SIXTEEN

"The Real Enemy"

THE MORNING CAME SOON. Instead of chickens or the seagulls that they had been hearing for some days had changed to crows. Their dreadful voices made everyone jump out of their places and run. There was no sign in the surroundings that it was morning. Everyone woke up very slowly. The breeze at the night had dozed off everyone's slumber.

With the resources gathered the previous day, they made a breakfast which was good enough for them. After that they all put on their armor and got ready to search the place.

"Alright, this time try to remain as a single group. Don't stray away from the others." The captain said to everyone.

Soon everyone headed into the dark jungle. With their swords up, Nicholas and Adrian were leading again. There were some strange creatures on the way. They were easily handled. They went on. The ground was full of grass and mud. There was also some small little bug like things.

As they moved on, things started to look clearer. The trees began to get colors. The sky started turning blue. Everything started regaining its colors. Soon, everything was back and looked the way how it should have looked.

"We should be careful now. We now approach their lair." Nicholas said and took the next step when Adrian saw something and stopped him.

There was a small sensor camouflaged in the mud. "You be careful." Adrian warned the captain.

"Look, we have found their place." John whispered to them.

Ahead, beyond a couple of trees was a clearing. They slowly approached it. Huge black walls stood like giants guarding whatever was behind them.

"We need to get a good look on those walls. Anyone got any ideas?" Adrian said.

One of Nicholas's men came forward "Here, take this." He gave Adrian a binocular.

"How did you get this?"

"Well, my job in Zandra was to sit at the crow's nest and look for new land. I always keep a binocular with me".

"Alright, let's have a look shall we?" Adrian took it and looked.

On the walls there were monsters standing guard. "I think I will have to climb a tree".

A little later he came back down. "Alright, there are two men each on all the four sides. There are huge gates on all sides too. Inside there are two towers with a monster on each with arrows and crossbows. Then there are two buildings. I think they are barracks and hold more monsters. In the very middle there is a small building in which I think Poseidon is being kept."

"So what should we do? Barge in?" John asked.

"No, we need to make a plan here." Nicholas said.

"Do we have any explosives?" Alex suddenly asked.

"Yes, sir. But some only. But that will be enough to destroy the fortification, sir. If that's what you are thinking."

"Thank you. So, we have ourselves a plan."

"What is it? Do share it with us too please."

"Okay. So first we have to blast the gate which is straight opposite to us. That will catch everyone's attention. At that point, my brother and I shall fly in. Two of you have to kill those guys in the tower, okay? Then we go in the building and get Poseidon out and once we have reached a safe distance, we shall fire up the place."

"It all sounds good in theory, but will it work?"

"Well, there's only one to find out".

They set to action. One of Nicholas's men set the explosives on the gate and came back "It is set, sir."

"Did anyone see you planting the explosive?"

"No, sir."

"Then we are ready to rock".

Alex and John climbed a tree and waited. Suddenly Adrian too came with them

"Wait, I have a better plan. How about I too sneak in silently and take out the guards one by one. In that way, it will be less and easier job for us."

"Well, in this case, you are our teacher. We have to follow you. What you say has to be right. Besides, I am starting to feel that my plan was a suicidal one."

"Okay. I have already said to Nicholas. He agreed with me. The only thing we need now is those guys in the tower to go down. Nicholas's men are on that."

As they watched, each of the monsters on the towers went down one by one. When it was made completely clear that the coast was clear, Alex and John silently flew in. They landed softly on the turf behind one of the barracks. One of the guards almost saw John when he landed.

Adrian also reached and led them. They tried to avoid the windows in the garrisons. They moved as quickly as possible. Adrian did most of the killing. Either he stabbed them or cut their throats. One by one they killed most of the monsters. They hid beside the tower when three guards were coming their way. Adrian told them to kill one each. When they approached, Alex and John got out from their hiding place and grabbed their necks. But instead of cutting the throat, they both stabbed them.

After killing them, they turned to see Adrian. He was just standing there. He didn't kill the third guard. They saw the guard running towards the barracks.

"What are you doing? You let him go?"

"Keep your voice down. I didn't let him go purposefully. The guy slipped off my hand. Let's just wait here and see what happens." He said in a calm voice as if he was not bothered about what was going to happen in a few seconds.

The monster ran straight into the garrison. After a few seconds, the alarm was sounded. Lot of monsters and creatures started coming out of the barracks with lances, swords and all. They were coming straight for the tower, exactly where the others were hiding.

Adrian came out with his swords without any shy. He called the others "Come on, guys. You're missing out the fun."

They had no other choice. They jumped out on the monsters and started razing them one by one. When they thought they had finished everyone, more started to come. Finally, after making their way through the enemy lines, they reached the central building. They fended off monsters for some time when Adrian said "Guys, you must go in and get Poseidon. I'll hold them off till then."

"You sure you can hold them off? I'm just asking."

Suddenly two other monsters just sprouted out of the floor. They looked hideous and tough too. They had huge swords and maces in their hands. They wore heavy armor too. Their eyes were blood red in color. They growled and snarled at the others and moved towards them.

Both of them flung their huge swords at them. It was by mere luck that they missed Alex and John. Moreover, their sword struck the ground and there was a huge crack on it. They did this a couple of times. Their swords were so heavy that they took some time to lift the sword up and hit again. This gave Alex and John an opportunity. Every time they dodged the monsters attack, they went behind them and attacked them. But their heavy armor made it impossible to land even a single scratch on their body. This continued on for some time. Surprisingly, the monsters didn't attack Adrian, who was watching the fight from a distance.

Suddenly when Alex and John were about to attack them, they quickly lifted their swords and turned to block them. They were taken aback. But not for long. In a moment they blocked the attack of the monsters. Both the brothers and the monsters were then hitting each other's sword with their own blades. At one point, Alex and John would be over the monsters and the other second, it would be the exact opposite.

Suddenly, when the monsters were almost on them, Alex and John felt so much energy infused inside them that they pushed away the monsters. The monsters were surprised. They fell down with a thud. John and Alex did not waste their opportunity. They quickly went and gave a fine stab to their chest. The armor then easily pierced. Some golden gas emerged from their mouths. This ensured that they were dead.

Alex and John sighed in relief. But they didn't have time for that. They still had to get Poseidon and get out of the place. They moved in as planned by Adrian earlier. They moved on. The building was small and there was only one cell in it.

They closed in on it. They broke the lock with their swords and went in. inside there was an old looking person. He had long beard and looked wearied out. When he saw them, he quickly recognized them.

"Alex and John! How did you find me?"

"Zeus sent us."

"Oh, he and his spies found me kept here! Great! Did you come here alone?"

"No, we came with Adrian and Nicholas. They are waiting for you out there. Come let's go."

They helped him up.

"Stop, did you say Adrian?"

"Yes, why?"

"You too fell into his trap! He is the reason why I was captured. He has betrayed us and joined enemy forces. Wait a minute. Is that Nemesis?"

"Yes, why should you . . ." John could not complete.

Nemesis slipped away from his hands and kept a distance from them.

"You old fool. Our plan was going out perfectly when you interrupted. You should have never come out, Poseidon." Nemesis said to the surprise of John and Alex.

"Plan, what plan? Will somebody please tell me what's going on here?" Alex said.

"Well, now that you are here you should hear. You fools. I am with Adrian. Do you think he is your friend? He is currently your enemy and Roark too is with me."

"Not "is" Nemesis, I am not with you. I have changed and I can't be enemy to these great fighting brothers. Look, Alex. Our true purpose was to spy on you, know your every move. It was Adrian who gave us to you to spy on you. He made Zeus and Poseidon believe that he will train you and give you swords. When we were given to you, we were actually one. Then we split. At that time, all the good inside us came to me and all the evil went to him. I wanted to tell you guys but then, Nemesis would know about it."

"But, why did you do this and Adrian too?"

"That's easy. We don't have to be chasing or be chased by monsters anymore. We will live the rest of our lives luxuriously as promised by Cronus while you shall rot in hell and die. In a few moments you shall die. You fools believed that Adrian also will enter inside. He had been with you all this time to see that you too die with Poseidon. He very well knew that you two can be killed only in Muspellheim" Saying this Nemesis rushed out.

Alex thought about the words of the old man and the oracle. How right they were. John shacked him suddenly "Come on, we can think about their treachery later, Right now, we have to get out of this place".

They ran outside. The monsters had gone. There was no Adrian. There was no Nicholas. There were no sailors. Only Roark was with them.

They were about to fly when they heard an explosion. It was coming from the other side of the building. They went to take a look. The final plan of Adrian and Nemesis to finish them all. They were sure that the entire area will blast any moment.

"Oh my god!! We have to get out of here. Come on."

Carrying the tired Poseidon, they flew with all their strength. They had made quite some distance but that was not enough. Alex thought about his primary element and concentrated. They were about to be caught in the blazing fire. But their element saved and it rained torrentially to save them from the huge fire.

CHAPTER SEVENTEEN

"The Reunion"

ALEX AND JOHN COULD not remember what happened after they flew from Muspellheim. Both were lying in a bed.

"Where am I?" John asked when got out of a bed.

Alex was lying beside him. He too woke up. They looked at their surroundings. They were in a wooden house. Through a window, they could see the sea. The house was on a beach. Suddenly, a man came through a door. They recognized him. The old man they met in the island where the volcano burst!

"Oh, you're up." He said in a soft but tough voice.

He poured something into two cups and gave it to them.

"What is this?"

"Don't worry. It will help you gain your senses."

They drank it. "Hmm, this stuff is good. Who are you? You look familiar and where is Poseidon?" Alex asked.

"That's good. You are beginning to remember. Do not worry. He's safe and back with Zeus."

"Where's Roark?"

"Oh, he's right beside you." It was true. The sword was there.

"John, you know now that Nemesis is gone. Nothing can be done about it. Don't be sad for Nemesis. He chose his own path."

"That's alright for me. But you didn't tell us who you are yet."

The man grinned "Alex, John, I am your father, Blake."

They took a moment to embrace the truth and they both hugged him. It was indeed a rejoicing moment for the father and his sons.

"My dear sons, your mission is only half done. It was my protection that saved you from Adrian's evil plan. But in Muspellheim, my protection had no power. But you both survived that too with your courage and power. You have been brought here to fight against Cronus as my plan could not be completed because of Adrian's cheating. Anyway, you may have to come again once I finish more ground work. Now I can meet Zeus again as he also believed Adrian that I cheated him and ran away with the diamond" he stopped for a while.

He continued "Soon you will be unconscious. Thanks to Poseidon and Zeus, you will reach your home safe as ever."

"But what about you?"

"I have more to do here. I have to find out the diamond stolen by Adrian to complete my plan to finish off Cronus. I can never return to earth anymore." Some tears started rolling down.

John and Alex were too sad to hear that and to speak anything.

"A few days of your future life you have spent here. So you will be lying unconscious when you reach there for a few days. You won't remember anything since you left your world. Roark will see that you reach your world and will return to me"

"But" Alex wanted to ask something.

"Listen my dear son . . . Don't worry. We will meet again . . . our mission is not yet over . . . whenever I need you, I will see that you reach me . . . . You will join me with all your powers again. Now it's time you to sleep . . . . It will be a long sleep . . . Good bye . . . ."

He hugged Alex and John and slowly they realized that they were fainting . . . And Roark was getting ready for his final mission for the time being . . . Hoping to help the great sons of Mr. Blake soon . . .